FAIRY TALE HORRORSHOW

Edited by
RJ ROLES & JASON MYERS

TABLE OF CONTENTS

Piper - M Ennenbach
Midnight at the Glass Slipper - Ruthann Jagge
Always Time for Tea - Natasha Sinclair
She Saw Red: Once Upon a Crime part 1 - Jason Myers
Swine of Another Kind: Once Upon a Crime part 2 - RJ Roles
Pinnochio the Wooden Hoe - Matthew A. Clarke
The Vengeful Little Mermaid - Tara Losacano
What Goes Into the Forest, Never Comes Out - Lance Dale
Tonight, Tonight - Denise Hargrove
It's No Fairy Tale Out There - Keven J. Kennedy

First and foremost, we'd like to thank the authors in the book you're about to read. After being messaged out of the blue with our crazy idea to put their own spin on beloved fairy tales, each one answered the call, going above and beyond with their imaginations. This is the first collaborative anthology for Crimson Pinnacle Press and we hope that you (the reader) enjoy it as much as we did. Another shout-out has to go to fellow author J.Z. Foster, who has always been there to help, whether with covers, or formatting, or questions we've had about how to do something. Lastly, there are two people who've always been there, waiting for whatever we have conjured on the page, to give us honest feedback, and catch those evil typos that try to find their way into the books. All our love to Marcie Robinson & Melissa Potter.

1

PIPER

(THE PIED PIPER OF HAMELIN)

M Ennenbach
Now

He sat alone at the mouth of the cave, angrily staring at the setting sun over the bustling town forming an artificial horizon at the other end of the valley. A haze of greasy smoke hung over the city, a funeral shroud filled with particulates that muddied the waning orange that painted the valley in shades of ember. If looks could kill, his scowl would erupt raining fires to ravage the town until all that remained was a black smear scarring the land.

"Hamelin," he muttered, not for the first time. His fists clenched so tightly his knuckles cracked and squeaks of fright carried out from the cave. "Nothing to be frightened of, my little ones. Just remembering the past."

Gleaming eyes reflected the setting sun; hundreds of softly glowing red eyes that watched him lovingly. He stood up and they parted for him—this mass of agitated yet now fed and docile rodents with long yellowed incisors, and long earthworm like tails—only to rush back together and follow as he ventured further into the dark. He looked at the torch in his hand and, with a practiced swipe of the flint, the tinder ignited the pitch-soaked cloth affixed to the charred wood. A drop of blue flame fell and a rat began flailing and rolling as the stench of burnt fur filled the mouth of the cave.

"Careful, little one," he said softly and gently patted out the flame lovingly, but his eyes never left the two skeletons, or the rats still fighting for the strings of rubbery meat and marrow the ever-gnawing mouths had finally chewed down to.

In the flickering light of the torch, the great swarm of rats seemed to move as one, just as he had painstakingly trained them to do. Rats aren't stupid creatures. History has (somewhat rightfully) painted them as vermin and carriers of plague. The church and common folk alike associate the poor creatures with evil, consorted them with witches (again, somewhat rightfully), and all manner of ill repute.

He saw them differently than the rest, though. He had grown up with them in that squat lean-to by the town dump. The so-called vermin had been better friends to the dirty little boy that lived there than the other children ever had.

He could hear the mocking voices, *"Pied Piper of the Dump, playing for his little rat family!"*

His foot reflexively lashed out and a half dozen rats went flying into the air with startled hisses. His eyes grew wide with panic and he exclaimed, "No! I'm so sorry, my pets!"

The rats were fine. Made up of solid muscle, they flopped and scrambled back upright and scurried back into the writhing horde. He shook away the taunting sing-song melody and ventured deeper and deeper into the warren of caves that interwove the valley, and eventually led to

Hamelin itself. When he first discovered the winding caves, he had been afraid to explore them. Rumors of kobolds and goblins, hidden kingdoms far beneath the surface, ran rampant in the town. Any time a new entrance was discovered, it was just as quickly collapsed. But he knew all of the hidden caves that littered the valley the townsfolk couldn't even imagine. And he was never alone. Not any longer, at least.

He reached his hand into his doublet with a feral smile and felt the worn ivory flute. That was a lesson he would never forget.

BEFORE

He would sit at the edge of the dump and play his wooden flute. No one minded the dirty boy, his father was busy tending to the garbage, and his mother had passed during childbirth—something both he and his father agreed was his fault. But he could play, and had a natural affinity for the flute. In any kingdom, in any other land, he would have been lauded for his talents. A virtuoso with zero training.

But not in Hamelin. He was just the filthy boy in a land of trash there. A living stain, the object of ire because of his sin of being born at the edge of filth and drowning in poverty. Other children were just as poor as he and his father, yet they looked down their noses at them as if proximity to the dump added gravitas to his situation and elevated their own. There was always worse, he just happened to embody the worst in Hamelin.

But children don't understand class divides, they just ape the mannerisms of their parents and use those building blocks to form a lifetime of preconceived ideas. His rats respect cunning and strength, not wealth. What is wealth to a rat? Plentiful food. Females to fuck. Broods to raise. Unafraid of the muck that makes up most of the world, they are masters at surviving.

He learned that from them.

When his father keeled over tending to the trash fires, he found himself alone at fourteen. As if the weight of the world's hatred was not enough to crush him, he now faced it alone. He wanted more than the dump. He wanted to be free. To play his flute and be showered with adoration.

He came up with a plan. When he first learned to play, he noticed the rats would all stop and stare when he played certain melodies. He didn't know the words, just had a gut instinct of how to manipulate the sounds. As his father shoveled shit from the streets, he would practice playing for the rats.

Rumors swirled of plagues in faraway lands, entire cities burnt to the ground. The strident faithful blamed the cats—clearly consorts of the Devil—and took to killing each and every one they saw. This led to the unbridled breeding of the rats, and soon the streets were teeming with yellowed teeth and beady eyes. The townsfolk cried out at their impending doom, and soon the Duke of Hamelin was faced with a problem. With no cats, how could they control the rats?

The call came and spread across the land, poisoners and rat catchers came from far and wide. No matter what they did, the rats always surged back in greater numbers. The Duke despaired of a certain plague that would reduce his duchy to a footnote in history.

And then he appeared. The Duke promised him a reward truly fit for a hero, as the townsfolk laughed at the nasty orphan from the edge of the dump—with his tattered clothes and hand carved flute.

But he showed them. He began at his shack, playing softly at first as the people snickered from their windows. But the laughter stopped as hundreds—thousands—of curious heads peered up from the trash. The rats in the streets, the alleys, on the rooftops, and swimming in the river took notice as well. The tune changed pitch, rising in intensity slowly. The heads stared mesmerized as their compact bodies moved of their own volition toward the enchanting melody. He strode past the now hushed homes, his fingers carefully sliding along the smooth wooden flute, and the swarming tide of matted fur undulated behind him down the winding streets.

The song echoed off of the buildings, so when he caught his breath, the sound still reverberated through tiny skulls. He marched triumphantly out the gates, which swung shut as the last wriggling form cleared them. Across the valley they moved until he finally let them go, back into the caverns beneath for the night, before heading back and knocking happily on the heavy wood.

The Duke himself stood on the walls to greet him. "You were as good as your word, lad! Well done."

He smiled proudly and bowed. "I have returned for my payment, good Duke of Hamelin."

The Duke began uproariously laughing at the now confused piper at the gates. The laughter multiplied, growing louder and louder as the townsfolk joined in. "You? A filthy rat from the town dump expects a reward? Here, take your reward, you ungrateful rodent!" the Duke yelled.

And the townsfolk began to rain garbage and excrement from the walls. He was bathed in trash, dripping in shit, as they all merrily laughed at his dismay. He turned and ran back into the valley. Back to the cavern where he played a new variation of the song. One of rage and revenge.

—

He had thought living in squalor as a human punchline had been his lowest point, but now, set adrift in the caverns, he discovered his rock bottom. It surprised him just how quickly he began to lose sense of himself—of his humanity—surrounded by rats in the mouth of this large cavern. His fear drove the rats mad, and he played the flute until his fingers cramped and his lips grew bloody in an attempt to try and appease the horde.

He was at the verge of exhaustion and he knew when he collapsed there was nothing but yellow teeth for the rest of his miserable, short time remaining. Food was short and they had already begun cannibalizing the weak. Fear became a motivator, every sharp note brought death closer. And it was in one of those missed notes he discovered a new way.

It was a variation, unplanned, on his concerto of calm, that burst into the echoing dark. One by one, the rats knelt in supplication and as he wearily moved the flute from his broken lips, that is how they remained. He slumped to the rocky floor and sobbed as part of his terror ebbed away. Only to be replaced by the sun setting behind the mountains and the shadows stretching into the cave. Across the valley—like the stars waking above—he watched the tiny flames flicker in the town. He could feel the fear changing and he was not sure he liked where it was turning. But as the lights in the town danced so far away, the boy that had nothing realized he had truly lost it all. His stomach grumbled and seemed to reverberate across the valley.

"Hail to you, Rat King," a soft voice whispered from within the cavern.

He leapt up in fear and turned to see a small figure; a shadow against the dark.

"Who's there?" he asked, ashamed at the quaver in his own voice.

The figure stepped out into the last rays of dusk and the

Piper let out a gasp. The newcomer was about three foot tall, and had long fur covered ears that reminded him of a rabbit. The thought of a rabbit brought on another loud rumble from his guts and he felt his face flush.

"I mean no harm, Rat King. My name is Flautis."

"You're a kobold!"

Flautis nodded. "That I am."

"But you speak common tongue."

Flautis laughed. "Men have forgotten much about kobolds and goblinkin since banishing us to the Below, it would seem. Yes, I speak the common tongue and many others, though, it is not often I have a chance to speak it. There are precious few *human* traders that venture down into the Below to peddle wares these days."

Piper looked at him in confusion. "What is the Below?"

Flautis smiled and gestured toward the cave. "Man has chosen his kingdom in the sun. Those of us that chose to survive went underground. Once, we shared the valley, goblin, kobold, and man. But eventually, the land of open skies became too small for man and his ego, in addition to the other races. We were driven below and slowly forgotten."

Piper looked confused. "Goblins and kobolds are monsters." His face flushed crimson again as he realized what he had said.

Flautis only laughed. "Says the young human covered in feces, commanding an army of rats!" Piper frowned and felt anger flare in his chest, but Flautis laughed again, and something in the gravelly laughter put him at ease. "Come with me, Rat King, and perhaps we can stop your stomach from grumbling."

"Where?" Piper asked suspiciously.

"My home, it is inside the cavern and carefully hidden. Your legion raised my curiosity and I came to investigate."

Piper looked at the rats, who seemed to be watching him

for orders. They seemed unperturbed by the kobold, indifferent even. He sighed and nodded, mistrustful, but hungry, and desperate enough.

Flautis smiled—his rodent-like face showing cracked yellow teeth—and reached into a small leathery satchel on his waist, pulling out a smaller bag. "Spit in your hand."

"Why? What is that?"

"You have every right to be suspicious, Rat King, but this is a mix of fungi that, if you spit onto and rub on your eyelids, will help to navigate the dark."

Piper just stared at him, unmoving.

"If I sought to harm you, I could have attacked when you sat staring at the city. You must learn to have faith if you are to learn to survive. My father used to say that to me when I was wee little." Flautis stood watching him expectantly. Piper spit onto his palm and Flautis poured a little powder into the pooled saliva. "Now mix it thoroughly and rub it onto your eyelids."

Piper did as he was bade, flinching as he massaged it onto his flesh. There was a slight tingle and he winced as the feeble starlight and fading sun blossomed into an explosion of light. He clenched his eyes tight and felt Flautis grab his arm and lead him into the cavern. He cast one last pained look at the city, and the now stabbing lights.

"Come on, Rat King! I have soup cooking and your rats can go scavenge!"

Piper stared in wonder at the inside of the cavern, a hidden spectacle that now radiated a blue effusion across the stone.

Flautis smiled as Piper took it all in. "Aye, lad, there is a world of beauty hidden below. You'll see. Come, it's this way."

They ventured deeper than Piper had ever dared before. Even with this starlight tinge to his vision, the foreign world seemed to press down upon him. Wonder ebbed to terror as he imagined the weight of the valley crumbling down and crushing him and the rats. Panic made his breathing harder, and the scurrying swarm sensed his anxiety in a ripple of alarm that spread quickly out. Flautis placed a reassuring hand on Piper's forearm, which startled Piper and set the rats to hissing warnings.

Piper forced himself to breathe.

The strange earthen smells flooded his nose with a cool dampness. He let it enter his system, eradicating the smell of shit and fear, the acrid scent of rat piss and the musky scent of Flautis. His heartbeat slowed; the thunder became a rumble, which in turn, became quiet. Somewhere, a steady drip from the fang of a stalactite into a pool, sounded like a metronome. Without thought, he put the flute to his torn lips and played a new melody that swirled around the stony fingers rising up from the floor, dancing upwards to wake the nesting bats, sending them from roost with the whooshing of wings. Flautis stepped back, fear now plastered on his canine countenance, as a tornado of bats spun above Piper who played on with no knowledge, simply lost in the song.

Once the spell was broken, both Piper and Flautis watched in wonder as the bats flew en masse out the tunnels, a cacophony of leathery wings soon fading except for the hollow echo reverberating through the Below; they continued to Flautis's home.

A bowl of stew turned into Piper staying on with Flautis and learning of the strange new land he had never once contemplated existing, much the less becoming his new home. Flautis taught him of the biomes and new flora and fauna. The rats—with whom Piper strengthened his bond and understanding of—began to clear out the more dangerous beasts such as bugbears and feral orcs. In time,

Piper truly began to feel at home in the darkness, Flautis had never judged him as anything less than Rat King, and the respect slowly cobbled together a new Piper from the broken young man that stumbled in, abandoned and banned from everything he had never known.

Flautis sensed a peace emanating from his charge. He would often sit in wonder and watch as Piper wove notes together, conducting a symphony of writhing forms to do his bidding. The rats tended to the fungus farms, and the bats began to roost above the plants at his command to supply guano to the plants. Flautis had been alone so long, he had forgotten the comfort of company. In Piper, Flautis found a friend. In Flautis, Piper found acceptance. Together, they found peace of a sort.

It was winter above when it all came apart.

At the beginning of his sojourn, Piper went to the surface at night to watch the lights of Hamelin at least weekly. As he grew more content, the trips became fewer and fewer. The above held nothing for him that the Below couldn't provide. Sometimes he dreamt of a damsel stumbling in and falling madly in love as he saved her from a cave troll, but he knew those dreams were the fantasies of a child. No woman would ever find her way to him, and he would never dare return to Hamelin. When these urges filled him with frustration at the things he could never have, he returned to stare forlornly at the lights. He was surprised to feel the cold as he ventured up, the snow whirling in the caves as he felt the frigid bite of winter air. He stood staring out over a valley painted white, the starlight still so bright to his eyes, unused to anything but the pale blue of the fungi he regularly applied to his eyelids, or the soft embers they used to warm their food.

He had no idea—as he stood blinking and shivering—that below him in the trees, a pair of hunters spied his silhouette and watched in wonder at the man that must be living in the cave. Instead, he went back down to his cozy home and slept, dreaming of maidens that would never come.

The next day he went off to explore. He and the rats had found a vein of emerald as thick as his thigh, and while he had no need for gems, it was a calm place to play an ode to the green he rarely saw. On the way back he smelled the heavy scent of pitch. He froze as he tried to recognize the smell assaulting his nose, thick and greasy in the stagnant air. Pitch meant torches, and torches meant man, his feverish mind put together as he began to run.

The small cave was in a state of chaos as he burst in. Embers smoldered on the floor and the various items Flautis and he had collected on their explorations lay in a pile next to Flautis, who was curled up in a ball. Piper ran over to his dearest and only true friend and felt the coolness of his skin. He rolled him over and saw his face had been badly beaten, and there was a stab wound—ragged and still dripping—in the center of his chest.

Something inside Piper snapped and he began to play an insidious dirge that intoned darkly throughout the cavern. The rats and bats stirred. The master's sullen rage infected the music and directed their small brains. He set them loose and chased after the swarm. They raced up and up, the scent of pitch growing stronger, joined by a salty musk of unwashed flesh. The music slowed and Piper strode forward alone—the barely contained fury of the horde palpable behind him—and cleared his throat to get the attention of the two men carrying large gems and chunks of gold in their greedy hands.

The men dropped the loot and turned in surprise. When they saw Piper, they relaxed a bit. One stepped forward, a thuggish brute with a jutting brow and coarse black beard to his belt.

"Aye boy, we seen ya yesterday and decided to have us an adventure. Killed us a monster as well, yer welcome."

They both laughed evilly before the other one—clearly a son or younger brother with the same features with only wisps of a beard growing in—spoke. "I bet you know where we can find more treasure, don't ya, cave urchin? How's about ya take us to some gems or something?"

Piper seethed internally, but smiled and nodded. He pulled a chunk of emerald out of his pocket, large enough to buy most of the duchy, and possibly the title of Duke as well, and showed it to them. "I just found a bunch of these, good sirs. If'n you truly killed a monster; it seems fair you are justly rewarded for your actions. Come, I will show you."

The men looked at each, eyes wide with greed and smiles that split their faces like axe wounds filled with grey broken teeth. They looked at Piper and nodded. "Carry on, our new friend," the elder said happily.

Piper smiled and bowed clumsily. "After you sirs, you have the torches to light our way."

The men didn't question why Piper didn't have a torch of his own. They let their greed override thought and began to strike flint to tinder to reignite their torches. It wasn't until they heard the first notes of the flute that they stopped and turned in fear.

The youngest pointed at him and drew his sword. "You're the rat boy! I remember flinging shit at you from the walls!"

The elder didn't say a word, he just held the torch into the darkness and stared as a rumble filled the air around them. He didn't have time to utter anything aside from a sound of surprise that morphed into a scream of terror, quickly silenced as the two were suddenly buried in a pile of yellow fangs, and black wings.

It took seconds before all that remained was gnawed bone. Piper snuffed out the torches and walked back to his home that was no longer. All he felt was hatred for those that had done nothing but take away his happiness. He planned. He knew the only way to prevent man from ruining his life any further was to eradicate them from the valley. From the entire planet.

But it would begin in Hamelin.

NOW

He stared at the torch, the fire like daggers in his eyes. He knew the city would be well lit, that rushing in blind would be his downfall. Piper played a mournful dirge that set the rats and bats into a frenzy, incrementally. He had tried to stomp out the hatred that wormed through his every thought, sought peace in the silence of the Below.

But he never stopped planning, never stopped preparing his army, never stopped needing his revenge. Flautis would have been disappointed to know just how deeply this need coursed through Piper. Flautis would have been sickened at the things Piper had done during his sojourns through the Below.

Flautis was dead though. Piper entered the cave and stared down at his mentor, his friend. At the only person to ever treat him as an equal.

"I'm sorry, my friend, but know I do it for us." Piper touched the torch to the papers spread on the floor beneath Flautis and turned away as they began to smolder on his roughspun tunic and ignite his fur.

Piper raised the ivory flute again, and this time, the tune thundered. The bats stopped aimlessly circling and grabbed tight to the stalactites, their small bodies quivered as they listened. The rats all stopped and formed a phalanx around Piper, the largest in an honor guard closest to the flute playing form in the dancing shadows of the torch hooked in his elbow. As one, they moved down the familiar corridor's etched from the stone long ago. It took them hours to reach the staging area at the far end of the valley. The stench of rot filled this smaller cavern situated directly beneath the dump itself, nearly bad enough to cover the bubbling green smoke that poured heavily out of a series of cauldrons seated over hot water springs.

With three sharp notes, a group of thirty smaller rats dove into the cauldrons. Another short song and they scurried up the walls of the cave and through the trash above. *I have trained them well*, he thought as he watched them. They would go to the main cistern and sacrifice themselves for the Rat King. Again, he repeated the song, with a slight variation in tempo. Another thirty dove and climbed to the surface, these going to the wells around the richer section of town, closer to the Duke's palace. Wave after wave of the tainted soldiers went to weaken the enemies of the town.

And then Piper allowed himself to stop, just for a little bit. He had to temper his anger and let the poison he flushed into the drinking water do its job. And he knew it wouldn't take long. On one of his excursions he had stumbled on a small village of kobolds, perhaps relatives of Flautis? Piper was never sure. He didn't bring them up, because he knew Flautis would disapprove of his testing the poisoned rats out in the small well of the village. Two rats had been enough to taint the water badly enough that, when he returned after a couple days, all that remained was the dead and dying kobolds.

He knew this would not take out Hamelin, but he figured it would be enough distraction to ensure eradication. He smiled as he thought of the kobolds twitching from his special blend of fungi and moss. The smile grew, and blood trickled from his torn lips, as he imagined the humans above suffering the same. These happy thoughts allowed him to sleep for a few hours.

When he woke, he climbed the narrow trail that wound its way up. He knew this trail like the back of his hand, having stumbled upon it as a child. He had never journeyed too far into the Below then, a sniveling filthy child in the total darkness. No, he didn't have that kind of bravery... then.

Now, filled with hatred and thirsting for revenge, he feared no creature. He carefully shimmied through a fissure in the wall—an easier task as a child to say the least—and froze as the dying rays of the sun played on the rock in front of him. It hurt his eyes, made them water, the setting sun far brighter than the feeble torchlight. The warmth of it—along with the scent of bread mixed into the trash odor he had grown up with—brought on a momentary sense of conscience. He paused, holding the flute up to his lips, and listened to the town, the endless noise of so many cramped tightly together. Retching and coughing carried loudly, Piper remembered the kobolds, remembered Flautis, remembered the men, the Duke, the shit; it all cascaded over his torn mind in waves of icy resolve.

As the last flickering rays of sun faded over Hamelin, a song began to carry over the town, and Hell itself was unleashed upon the unsuspecting townsfolk.

Geysers of trash erupted, as the bats burst into the sky blotting out the stars and moon above. Screams erupted as the cloud of claws and teeth descended upon the people frozen in panic. Then, the rats exploded in wave after wave of coiled evil intent. Piper played faster and faster, infuriating the already ravenous host of rodents, spinning them deeper and deeper into maddening hunger and need for blood. The guards on the wall closest to his entrance from the dump identified him quickly and began to fire volley after volley of arrows. Piper ducked behind a building, ignoring the hail of metal tipped death tearing through the thin walls and carefully wound his orchestral maneuver of death.

Rats surged up the wall and, one by one, the arrows ceased to fly as the guard's screams joined the people in the streets. Piper strode down the street, his honor guard always close, snapping and attacking any that dared approach him. Around him, chaos took over as hundreds of thousands of rats were driven mad with bloodlust and his song tore through walls and overtook entire buildings in mere seconds. He paused his song, the effects already deeply seated into the small brains of his army. Through lowtown, the unstoppable army marched, leaving nothing but wreckage behind them. Piper watched a man fleeing the surging swarm only to trip and lay screaming. A tidal wave swept over him—a mere lump beneath an ocean of clambering claws and teeth—until all Piper saw was a smear of red with bits of bone on the cobblestone streets. All the way to the gates of hightown, Piper and his furious horde of bats and rats went, bloody skeletons and the corpses of his fallen troops lined the roads.

Piper stopped far enough from the closed gates to hightown to be heard, but not shot by the guards standing with torches staring in horror at the carnage of lowtown.

"Bring me the Duke, along with my payment for services rendered!" Piper yelled.

He watched the guards look nervously at one another, knowing the gates were no defense against an army that could fly and climb. Piper stood nonchalantly with his back against one of the still standing walls of what used to be a pawn shop. He remembered it well, his father had sold off his mother's gold tooth and family ring for mere pennies to buy booze. Cold gripped at his heart as he forced himself to appear calm.

"Rat Catcher?" the Duke called from the wall. "It has been

two long years we have awaited your return for payment! I apologize for our little prank before, it was meant to be hilarious and honor you!"

Piper spit blood onto the street and laughed, a sound devoid of any humor at all. "A joke? Was it simply a joke?"

The Duke nodded. Piper could imagine his chins wobbling as he did so. "A misunderstanding, a jest in poor taste! We can right this wrong! Name your price and it is yours!"

"Anything I want?"

"Yes! Spare me and my people and I will even give you my duchy!"

Piper laughed again. "And what need does a king have for a duchy?"

The Duke laughed this time. "A shit-covered commoner dares to consider himself a king?"

Piper stepped forward, just out of where he gauged arrow distance, and bowed. "I am the Rat King! My price is the lives of all of Hamelin!"

A twang sounded and Piper felt something punch him in the stomach. He fell to the ground and stared at a footslength of wood sticking out from a growing crimson stain on his shirt. The Duke laughed again, and Piper heard the gates begin to raise slowly. "Get him! A hundred gold marks to whomever brings me the head of the Rat King!"

Piper cringed from the pain, but raised the flute to his lips and played a song he had only ever dreamt before. His army raced beneath the rising gate and over the wall. But as he played through gritted teeth, his honor guard began to circle him. Two large rats ran up his legs and wrapped themselves around his forearms, tails tightly constricting, and claws digging in deep. Piper ignored the pain in his guts as more of his guard climbed his flesh and attached themselves to his body. He felt his limbs lose strength, but the rats kept him standing. More and more wrapped themselves around him until he was no longer a man, but a true Rat King.

He ran forward, the rats moving as one being. A living swarm with a hive mind controlled by the song of his ivory flute. His new body climbed the wall effortlessly as the song continued to play and draw more and more rats onto his writhing form. He leapt off of the wall and raced down the blood-soaked street. Arrows punched into the rats and as one fell, two took its place. He couldn't hear the screams as his forces tore through hightown, all he cared about was the coach racing to the palace of the Duke.

The skies above Hamelin were filled with flapping leather wings and the cries of the dying as Piper tore apart any human foolish enough to stand before him. A troop of guards rushed out to at least try and slow him down so the Duke could get to safety. Piper threw himself into the guards, his constantly shifting suit of rats lashing out against the armored men. It took moments to leave nothing but bloody metal and splintered bones.

Again, Piper ran, nestled inside this cocoon of rodents as his blood slowly poured to the street. He played faster and faster, spurring on the rage driving his own failing body and those of his rats. Soon he found himself at the palace itself. His army poured inside, the last safe bastion left standing in the great town of Hamelin. Piper turned back to see hightown in ruins, spires of flame and carnage covered everywhere he looked. The sky filled with wings, the streets and roofs still standing with red eyes reflecting the fires and blood.

Fading as he was, Piper played on and on as the Rat King stepped into the palace to see a sea of red, with strewn intestines littering the polished floors. Piper ignored the yelling guards, his rats overtaking any foolish enough to stand before him. The portraits that lined the walls were splinters and torn canvas, the furniture reduced to rubbish soaking in blood as he strode to the heart of the palace.

And there he found the Duke, standing on his throne, wailing a high-pitched sustained sound of insanity and loss. Piper played a quick flourish and the rats detached themselves from him and he nearly crumpled to the ground if not for a few of his loyal guards keeping him upright.

"And now for my payment, Duke," he called out hoarsely." The Duke didn't stop his wailing as the rats encircled his throne, snapping and hissing at him. Piper watched for a moment, feeling robbed at the final act of his revenge. He felt the flute drop from his deadened fingers and all he could do was point and let out a strangled whistle.

It was enough.

As darkness encroached the edge of his vision, he saw his family, his loving servants, his soldiers, begin to chew their way up the Duke until all that was left exposed was the dying man's face, still wailing until one final choke silenced him. A large gray rat burst through his throat and out of his mouth in a shower of gore.

Piper smiled as his guard lowered him to the ground. He looked around, but didn't see the palace in tatters. Instead, he saw the cave and Flautis sitting in his favorite chair. Flautis spoke, but strain as he could, Piper could not make out the words. He tried to speak, but no words came, only a bright red bubble that popped soundlessly. He reached out, and one of the smaller rats pushed the ivory flute into his hand, so familiar to his grip, like another appendage.

And then the world went dark, darker than the Below.

The End

MIDNIGHT AT THE GLASS SLIPPER
(CINDERELLA)

Ruthann Jagge

Her hair is matted and tangled. The beautiful young woman wears only a ripped tee-shirt, covered in filth. She yanks hard at the chains locking her bruised feet together. It hurts too much to do it again. He doesn't bring her water anymore, let alone food. Maybe if she gets thin enough, the metal clamps around her ankles will slip off. Or she will die; it isn't the worst thing that can happen. There's a pile of expensive shoes in the middle of the concrete floor. Some have brown stains, and one pair looks coated in fresh blood. An industrial garbage bag partially covers the remains of another young woman, and the flies are hungry.

—

ELLY CYNDERS STRUGGLES up the narrow steps with a heavy crate of cheap glasses. She shares her makeshift living space, consisting of an army cot and a few plastic bins, with cases of beer and towers of paper towels stacked against the walls. The floor of the Glass Slipper is sticky with spilled beer, and she isn't anxious to experience the condition of the restroom. Friday nights are always busy. Using her hip, she pushes the heavy cellar door open, getting ready for the start of business at 2:00 pm.

"He got another one." Sparkly Ed, a regular who favors sequins, bursts through the front door as soon as Elly unlocks it. He's wheeling a duffle bag behind him. "Grabbed a coffee, and folks are buzzing; they found two severed female feet in the park this morning. Feet. Who the hell does that, and where's the rest of her?" Ed's unusually fair skin looked silver in the daylight. He's a lovable sometimes-actor who makes everyone feel special.

Elly wipes the bar. The worn wood is scarred and covered in graffiti. Dozens of hastily scrawled messages suggest "a good time" and "for hire" with phone numbers and names. Patrons are looking for something they want or need. She pours Ed—wearing blue sequin pants in honor of Saturday—a beer on the house.

"It's the second time this month." Elly smears back her blonde hair, recently chopped short, with her wet hands. A customer played with matches and burned off an inch by accident when a pile of cheap napkins flared up in her face. The quick actions of Joey the Rat, a respected bookie, saved her when he dumped a cold glass of foamy draft over her head. Elly cares more about the Glass Slipper, the small neighborhood bar she manages. Her hair will grow back.

The crumbling brick building is old, in need of a facelift

and new windows. The place belonged to her dad, and it's all she has left of him. The hours are long, and the work rough, but the regulars are the family she chooses, so she makes the best of it. Officer John Cynders died last year during a drug deal gone bad. Elly works hard at keeping his memory alive. John invested in the property so his friends and folks he met on the job would have a safe place to be when life gets hard. Elly appreciates her customers; lost souls, lonely cops, and colorful characters who hang out on cracked leather stools next to each other along the weathered bar, sipping, chatting, and solving problems. Live and let live, and despite their flaws, these folks are decent humans. Sparkly Ed points at a bottle of whiskey, nervously tapping on his empty glass.

"Sorry, Elly, I'm upset. I don't know what's out there, but my gut tells me none of us are safe. I'm not sacrificing a perfect pedicure to some freak who cuts off feet." Sparkly Ed gulps the liquor down. The pretty blonde girl nods. She's scared too; no one deserves death by chopping. Elly blocks out terrible images flashing through her mind.

"It's awful, and I hope they catch them soon. The feet and sometimes other parts show up. I don't want to think about the person doing these things."

"You need someone to keep you safe." Ed winked.

"Maybe so, but who has time or energy to find one? One wrong move, and my stepmother will put me out on the street." She tosses the bar rag into a bin and grabs a clean one, polishing the freshly washed glasses.

Glancing at the neon clock without the number "9", Elly guesses her stepmother, Gillian, will be in soon to collect the substantial week's rent in cash, along with any expensive bottles of liquor that catch her eye. The arrogant woman is an experienced con artist, and a skilled liar. She pretends to be respectable. Elly puts up with her criminal stepmother out of loyalty to her father. The woman shows her no kindness.

She left college during her senior year when her beautiful artist mother, Angela, died tragically in a car accident. She put her dream of a career in medicine on hold, moving home to look after her grief-stricken father. John wasn't one to clean or cook a meal for himself, and he needed her. They were close and comforted each other through the terrible loss. He met Gillian a few months later during a routine eviction. She and her two spoiled daughters lived in a plush uptown condo under a false name, supporting a luxurious lifestyle on stolen credit cards, shoplifting, and fraud. John was assigned to serve her legal papers, but she charmed him with sob stories and her fabulous figure. Soon after, John asked the stunning redhead to marry him. He could offer her security and wanted a family again. Elly wanted her dad happy, so she rearranged rooms and her heart to make space for Gillian and her daughters, Amy and Sally, who moved into her home, demanding fresh décor and expensive new furnishings along with entirely new wardrobes.

John Cynders wasn't a typical cop; his grandfather designed valuable software, eventually selling it for millions. His only grandson was the primary heir, but John chose a career in law enforcement over his grandfather's affluent lifestyle. He married his high school sweetheart, Angela, and together they built a wonderful home full of laughter and fine art. Elly was born into an easy life, and her parents focused on music and education, travel, and charitable causes. She and her mother visited museums and took ballet classes, while John fought crime; his girls dragged him away for fun every chance they could. John doted on his blonde daughter, who loved the color pink. He made sure she could protect herself with confidence and encouraged compassion for those less fortunate. He called her "Princess", but insisted she be humble and gracious.

Elly smells funeral flowers before the door—badly in

need of new hinges—flies open. Gillian Cynders and her daughter, Sally, slither in wearing tight jeans, silk blouses, and designer sunglasses. Gillian's green shirt sets off her dyed red hair, and Sally is flashy in bright yellow with the ends tied high above her sculpted abs. Her youngest stepsister, Amy, is a mess, with her smeared-eyeliner attitude, wearing fuzzy cat ears above her headphones. Gillian sets her expensive handbag on the bar, wrinkling her nose in disgust. Over the top of her glasses, she stares at her stepdaughter's practical black leggings and stout black ankle boots. A tightly laced sky-blue satin corset over a sheer white blouse accents her tiny waist, which also helps to support her back during the long hours on her feet. Thick leather cuffs on both wrists protect her skin from broken glass, and silver hoop earrings gleam under her cropped hair. A rhinestone clip shaped like a tiara twinkles over one ear.

"I see you're going for a slutty bar-wench look today. Or maybe a damsel in distress?" They all laugh. Sally flips her hair dramatically.

"Elly, do you ever clean this shithole? It smells like wet dog and bad decisions in here." Sally grabs a handful of napkins, wiping her shoes as she swivels into a seat. Sparkly Ed turns to the polished brunette.

"Nice shoes. I bet whoever's out there would love adding them to the collection, but I suspect they're more interested in chopping your tootsies off. Overpriced stilettos already have their ticket to hell." Ed karate chops the air, holding his glass up for another pour. Sally gawks at the thin man wearing blue sequin bell bottoms. Elly's lips curl in a half-smile. Sally is the least intelligent female in her extended family. Snippy Amy shrugs her headphones to her shoulders, eager for a fight.

"Yeah, so they found another pair of feet, no big deal. The

salon was in a panic this morning. I'm in a hurry, Elly, stop wiping and pay the rent."

Gillian opens her bag, grabbing the bills her stepdaughter hands over. "This feels light. I hear you're doing good business on the weekends. I'm raising the rent by a thousand dollars next week." Setting her diet soda on the bar, she glances at her gold watch. Elly is stunned. She turns away to make a pot of coffee, not giving the woman the satisfaction of a tear.

They were married only a couple of months when John died, but Gillian immediately produced a will, claiming his fortune. According to her team of greedy attorneys, his untimely passing made Elly second to his new wife as executor of his estate. Gillian and her girls wasted no time removing every trace of her father from the house, hiring an expensive decorator with plans to expand the garden and construct a theater room.

"I suggest you find another place to live. This house isn't big enough for you to stay here." Gillian pointed to three suitcases lined up in the hallway of Elly's home. "I've packed your clothing, and the girls took the rest of your mess to a thrift store, although, I can't imagine anyone would want those... *things*." Elly dug her fingernails into her palms, struggling to understand.

"Why are you doing this? I don't care about the money. I'll stay out of the way and go back to school as soon as I can." Her stepmother kicked at one of the cases.

"I hope you can pay for it. You won't get a dime from me. Go live at that nasty bar your father thought was so special. I have no use for it. You will, however, pay rent, and if you're so much as an hour late, I will sell it so fast your head will spin. Stop whining and make yourself presentable. You look ridiculous in those clunky boots. They remind me of your awkward father and his tacky uniform."

Sparkly Ed opens his mouth to give Gillian a piece of his mind, but Elly pats his hand and replaces his glass with a steaming cup of coffee. Amused, she watches Amy slide the roll of bills from her mother's purse into her backpack while Gillian pats her hair, admiring herself in the long mirror behind the bar.

"Fine. Whatever you want. Please leave," Elly insists before it gets ugly.

"Oh, did I mention we're having an event tonight? Collectors and investors will be there. My girls are very excited, no doubt they'll meet future rich husbands." Gillian stops at the door behind Sally and Amy. "You will make an appearance. They're coming to buy the awful paintings hanging all over my house. You will smile pretty and make damn sure they get sold, or you'll be looking for another nasty place to live—seven o'clock. Don't come looking homeless and poor. Oh wait, you are." Gillian laughs so hard she trips, and Sally and Amy prop her up, also laughing hysterically. Ed slams the door hard behind the shrill females climbing into the waiting car

Defeated, Elly slumps over the bar as the door bangs open again. A pair of seasoned gangsters, Joey the Rat and Billy Bird, stroll in with their muscle, Hamburger Mike and Big Mo. They all tolerate Ed, who claps Joey on the back laughing when the short man bites the end of a large cigar, asking what the hell is up with his sequin pants. Bill runs a limo service and protects a team of upscale escorts. Joey, the notorious bookie, funnels their cash into legitimate accounts, dodging taxes and lazy live-in boyfriends.

"You heard? More feet," Billy greets Elly, but the young woman is melting down.

"What's up, Doll? Why the waterworks?" Billy's eyes narrow, Hamburger Mike moves in on high alert. Sparkly Ed scrambles behind the bar, taking Elly's arm.

"Sit. We'll help. Don't let that smelly hag get to you." Ed stokes Elly's hair, guiding her onto a barstool.

"It's too much. I barely make rent, and the basement's awful. I hate living down there. I'm tired and have no time off. Now the bitch wants more. I can't go to her fancy party. I don't have anything nice to wear, she'll end up selling everything, and I don't want to lose this bar. Dad loved it, and my real family is here." Joey and Billy surround them, tapping on their phones.

"I got you." Joey the Rat holds up his screen. "It's waiting for you at *House of Fashion,* my treat, Sweetheart. You're about a size six, right?"

Elly sniffs into a napkin. The blue dress in the photo is dreamy. She nods her thanks at the short man with dark whiskers near his nose.

"You need nice shoes." Billy Bird's fingers fly. "The girls I look out for shop here; the guy who runs it imports expensive designer stuff." Billy points to the screen with a nicotine-stained finger. Elly blows her nose, giving him a small smile. "Wash your face, I have a plane to catch, but a car is on the way. They close at five." She hugs the two men tightly.

Ed takes her hand, cocking his head to one side. "I can't afford to chip in, but I'm amazing with hair and makeup." Elly kisses his cheek, and he blushes. "There's not much time. I can work my magic in the car."

"You go with her. Get whatever she needs. I'll keep an eye on the place, but be back at midnight. I'm never late with the daily payouts. You can close up after." Joey the Rat pulls a thick blue rubber band from a bunch of celery off a fat wad of cash, handing most of it to Ed. The unlikely stylists wave Elly and Sparkly Ed—and his rolling bag—out the door into a shiny black limo with tinted windows.

"Punkin' Pete will take you. Remember, midnight." The limo, driven by a round man with rosy cheeks, glides away.

—

THE SCREAMING IS RELENTLESS, and the sound of power tools grinding, and squealing make her sick to her stomach. Nothing comes up, and she's dizzy. The girl claws at the steel links—shattering her remaining fingernails—but it's useless. There's a sliver of light as a door opens above the uneven wooden stairs she's chained beneath. A heavy object bumps down, landing close to her. The blood from a headless, footless, female body spurting red blooms like a bouquet of roses at her feet. She gives in to the darkwave and passes out.

—

"LOOK AT ME, ELLY." Ed opens his bag, covered in random theatrical stickers. Digging, he hands Elly a box of wipes. "I have enough stuff in here for an army. You're gorgeous and don't need much."

She cleans her hands and face, grateful for her friends. Ed applies her makeup; he's skilled from years of backstage work. He adds a swipe of smoky shadow, a bit of glow. Deep wine lipstick pops the lovely girl's blue eyes. She is flawless.

"Want to take a look?" Ed holds up a small mirror, Elly is delighted. He works a bit of hair cream between his long fingers, then reaching over, he expertly styles her short hair.

"I like the tiara clip, it sparkles, and I don't have extra

jewelry on hand." He replaces the bauble over her ear, pleased with his work.

Pete parks the car near a tiny boutique in the best part of town. A display of fabulous high-heeled shoes fills the window.

"I'll get the dress, and you can change on the way. Be right back." Sparkly Ed slides over as Elly climbs out. The sleek black vehicle speeds away as she pushes the doorbell.

Damn, it's after five already.

Walter Prince isn't expecting anyone. He only accepts clients by appointment. The slick man in a suit considers opening the door for the blond girl with her nose pressed against the glass. She's the last one. He intends to leave town soon.

"Hi, I need something for a party. I don't have much time." Elly storms into the luxurious showroom. Walter looks her over, staring at her low-heeled black boots. The laces are untied and dragging on the floor.

"I'm Mr. Prince. What's your size, Miss?" Elly plops down onto an upholstered couch. "I think I'm a seven, maybe eight? Depends."

Walter opens a box, carefully folding back crisp tissue, and removes a pair of silver shoes with exceptionally high heels. Tiny crystal stars dance on the toes. Elly pulls off her worn boots; she's excited to try them on.

"Wow, what beautiful shoes." Walter kneels, and as she slides her foot in, he closes his eyes, breathing deeply. Her feet are perfect. Elly takes a few steps, bending to admire them.

"I'll take them. My friend, Ed, is coming with money." She nestles the shoes back into the box.

"I have another pair you might like better. Let me show you." Walter holds out his hand, helping her up. She feels like royalty. "They're in the backroom, right this way." He guides

Elly toward a curtain hanging near the counter, tightly holding her hand.

Walter quickly pulls the curtain to one side. There's a door behind it. He kicks hard, and when it flies open, he shoves Elly down a set of steps. She screams, grabbing air as she falls. Walter slowly descends behind her.

"What the hell is wrong with you?" Elly scrambles to her bare feet. She's not hurt. Her eyes quickly adjust to the low light. There's a metal shelf with large glass jars standing against the wall and a pile of shoes in the middle of the room with a rough cement floor. It smells awful. "I'm leaving. Get out of my way." Walter blocks the only exit.

"You're the last, and the best; your feet are perfection. My collection will bring joy to whoever finds it." Walter points to the jars. Severed female feet float in clear liquid, and beautiful heads with open mouths scream silently from within. Elly inches back, she hears metal scraping along the floor. The dark-haired girl under the stairs pulls frantically at her chains, shaking her head wildly, trying to loosen the scarf tied over her face.

"This is Lola, a dear customer. She's almost perfect, but your feet are even more delicious." The girl throws herself against the wall. "I planned to bring her with me to my new place." Walter leers at the girl, then stomps hard on her leg. Lola whimpers. "Now, you'll get to watch me add her to my collection before we leave together." Reaching under the stairs, he pulls out a molded plastic case. It contains industrial power tools. "Hope you aren't delicate. It will get messy. Let's calm you down first." He moves closer to Elly, but she lands a solid punch to the side of his head, and his knees buckle. The blonde rips the rhinestone clip from her hair and jams the points of the tiara into his left eye. Walter screams as dark blood sprays.

"You're dead now. I wanted you to be my princess." He

clutches his eye, trying to grab a tool from the case, but Hamburger Mike and Big Mo bang down the steps. Mike effortlessly puts Walter in a headlock, squeezing the breath out of him.

"You okay, girl? Ed came right back, but the door locked on a timer. He saw this piece of shit push you around through the window. Punkin' Pete hit the panic button in the car. Mo and I are always ready." The huge men wearing tailored suits are furious. Mo saws through the chains securing Lola's ankles, gently lifting the crying girl into his arms. She leans into him, pulling at his tie and murmuring thanks. His eyes are soft.

"She's hurt. She needs food and a doctor." Elly takes her hand.

"No hospitals, I got a doc on call. My guy will fix her right up." Mo nods at Mike then carries Lola up the stairs with a plan.

Walter Prince is curled up on the floor, still locked in Mike's grip, blood pouring down his face. Hamburger Mike looks around the room. "What the fuck? He's the freak leaving women's feet all over town. Fuck me, are those heads? Poor girls, you gave them a world of hurt. It's your turn now, asshole." Mike chokes Walter harder. "Leave now, Elly. I'll take care of him, then call a cleaner. They'll find all this soon enough. It's not my area. I got work to do. They don't call me Hamburger Mike for nothing." Reaching into his pocket, the big man pulls out a steel multi-tool, snapping it open. Walter Prince wails and thrashes as Mike sinks a corkscrew into his cheek, biting off an ear. Elly gags, running up the steps. Ed is at the door, catching her as she drops in his arms. The gold sequin scarf wrapped around his neck sparkles. He is magic.

"What time is it?" She whips her head around, looking for a clock.

"You're safe. Let's go home. It's after ten, and it's too late." Ed leads her to the car.

"Did you get the dress? I have to go to Gillian's, or I will lose the bar. Don't try to stop me." Tires squeal as Pete speeds away from the mess. He's on the phone.

"We got her. It's all good."

Elly unlaces her corset and pulls her blouse over her head. Ed lowers his eyes, handing her a zippered bag protecting the fancy dress hanging inside. She slips it on. The wisp of blue silk fits her perfectly. Sparkly Ed fluffs her hair and dabs on fresh lipstick as Pete pulls up to the elegant mansion Gillian claims to own. A large white tent covered in tiny twinkling lights is packed with beautiful people, chatting and admiring many paintings propped up on easels. Elly recognizes them. Some are her mother's work, and one is a portrait she painted of her as a child. She wipes away a tear, walking barefoot on the thick grass of the manicured lawn.

"Elly, how disgusting. No shoes? You are a cellar rat." Gillian is wearing a tight red dress, clutching the arm of a much younger man with a loose bun on top of his head. Sally and Amy snicker behind her. Both are stumbling drunk. "I warned you to arrive early and sell this crap." Gillian tosses her glass of champagne at the girl. "Get out of here. You're nothing but bar trash, and you aren't welcome!" Wiping at her ruined dress, Elly turns to leave, almost knocking over a man standing behind her. The incredibly handsome gentleman is wearing a tuxedo and a friendly smile.

"So sorry." She wants to run. Ed's waiting in the car, and it's late. "I didn't mean to bump into you." Tears stream down her face.

"Hi there, I'm David Wright. Will you walk and look at the art with me? I'd like to buy it all for my private collection. There is a painting of a young lady wearing a pink dress with ruffles. She looks a lot like you. Can you show me around?"

His dark eyes glitter. Whispering and giggling, Sally and Amy cling to him on either side, but he holds out his hand to Elly. His assistants quickly remove her stepsisters—stinking of alcohol—as Gillian slowly claps, mocking her stepdaughter.

"No. I'm leaving. Nice to meet you." Elly runs across the damp grass. The man intently watches the black limo speed down the road. Elly's future is uncertain. The clock on the dashboard reads midnight.

"I was worried." Joey the Rat is holding court at the Glass Slipper, entertaining a few regulars with stories of the good old days of organized crime, when Sparkly Ed and Elly arrive. "I got details from the boys, sorry for the trouble. I'm off to work. Mo's staying with your friend Lola. Mike's waiting for me." The small man pats Elly's shoulder on his way out, just another day in the life.

"I can stay if you want?" Ed is exhausted, and the adrenaline rush is over.

"No, I'm closing up and going to bed. My nightmares are calling. Thanks for everything, see you soon." She hugs him goodbye.

A greasy little man hands Elly an eviction notice two days later; she has thirty days to vacate. She's decided to return to school. Joey the Rat and Billy Bird will pay her tuition and expenses. She calls them "Uncle" now, and they smile. She plans to throw a farewell party on the night of her birthday next week. Sparkly Ed is in charge of the menu and music.

The Glass Slipper is standing room only on the night of the party. A DJ spins by request, and Elly is very busy behind the bar, but Lola is helping. Hamburger Mike and Big Mo are at the door making sure Gillian and her monsters don't get in. A grey-haired man in glasses pushes his way up to Elly.

"Miss Cynders?" She leans over to hear him. "I'm Alex de Gouse, Attorney. Hate to bother you. It's a great party." Elly's forehead wrinkles, and he notices the rhinestone tiara clipped over her ear. He fans several papers out on the bar. "I'd like your signature. Your father set up a private trust payable on your twenty-first birthday. You're a wealthy young woman, my congratulations." Elly glances at the papers, and the amount, and screams in excitement. Mike and Mo are at her side in a flash.

"I won't lose the Glass Slipper. Now I can own it outright." Elly scrawls her name and shakes hands with de Gouse, who leaves immediately. Sparkly Ed carries over a massive bouquet of white roses, setting them on a table near the bar.

"For you, they just came." There's a card tucked into the glossy leaves.

"Happy Birthday to my favorite painting. I'd love to share your memories." Signed, David Wright. There's a phone number on the back of the card. Elly tucks it in her bra, delighted.

—

THE ANIMAL CAGE IS SMALL. Sally and Amy can't sit or lie down comfortably. Dirty red shop rags soaked in gasoline are shoved deep into their mouths, and they've peed themselves repeatedly. What's left of Gillian's naked body is tied to a table in the center of the room. Her red hair lies in a heap on the floor. She can't scream anymore.

"Almost finished. Who's next?" Hamburger Mike grins at the sisters. He's holding a pair of electric lawn clippers dripping with blood. Joey the Rat and Billy Bird strongly disagree with Gillian's treatment of Elly. Her Dad was a good guy and played fair. They decide to take care of the problem once and for all. The old men sent Big Mo over to Gillian's with a van full of upscale designer clothes as a "thank you gift" for their treatment of Elly. When the three women swarm like angry bees in the back of the truck, demanding more and better, Mo slams the double doors closed in a done deal. Elly will never know.

"I hear your step-shits relocated to Paris?" Sparkly Ed is thrilled Elly is home from med school for a couple of days. The Glass Slipper serves lunch now, and business is booming. Lola runs the bar, and Big Mo waits for her every night at closing time.

"Yes, sometimes there's a postcard. I don't have a return address, but I hope my so-called family is gone for good." Elly kisses her friend. "See you later. I'm meeting David. We're planning a fundraiser for the museum." Ed waves her away.

—

"WHAT KIND of music do you like? Me? I like classic rock. I work better with good bass." Hamburger Mike replaces his noise-blocking headphones and pounds in another nail. He always enjoys his work.

The End

3

ALWAYS TIME FOR TEA
(ALICE'S ADVENTURES IN WONDERLAND)

Natasha Sinclair

Alicia's fingers danced gingerly over the stiff structures of her exoskeletons. Lined up—exquisite high-fashion, high-function—soldiers ready for their queen's command. Which armour would she pick today? Each of these fine garments had its own unique story and bestowed upon her the essence of their life-force when her body was tightly cocooned within, tight-laced in finely seasoned disciplined bondage. This part of her morning ritual, eyeing down the line of her extraordinary closet, set her up for any adventure that may present.

Choosing her costume made her head rush with desire. Sometimes murderous, often deviant. These carefully constructed bones elicited nostalgia, in keen euphoric waves, when her fingers danced, pulling her palm in for a full-snug grasp. The memories of each wearing would wash over her, full sensory explosions—scent, sight, taste, and technicolour illustrations painted in her mind, her dreams; nightmares, coming to life. Lovers and submissions unfolded within her.

Today's chosen garment was an intensely deep claret, a replica of an old favourite. Her very first cinched in at Twenty-two inches closed—now fifteen inches was her cinched maximum, and today she craved the comfort of that unrelenting restraint. She performed her first ritualistic "ring" exchange of dedication on Lupercalia wearing this very construct (then at twenty-two inches). This dedication was as much to oneself as it was to the other two. Her strong four-poster bed was centred on top of the hand-engraved Baphomet pentagram adorning the solid wood floor, inconspicuously covered by her antique tartan rug. This space was sacred, as every ritual conducted upon it held intent, whether singular, or unity of multiples.

She was first to submit to the needle. Laying down on black latex sheets, head nestled between Red's thick, warm fishnet wrapped thighs—the back of her hands gently placed in Red's large open palms. Alicia tight-laced, her breathing was shallow in the strict confines of the silk and steel. Her fishnet stockings hugged her legs to the pale exposed upper thigh, the alabaster gateway to her neatly trimmed cunt. As he soulfully kissed her toes, sucking tenderly through the nets, slowly making his way up her legs toward the passage of all life, of deathly sweet ecstasy. Shallow breaths, growing fast with every movement of him on her. He reached the naked part of her thighs and used his large palms to spread her legs further apart. The cool air from the ajar window rushed over her exposed lips like airwaves of mint, refreshing, clean, and ready.

Chess teased her just a little before pushing his shaft inside and rising over her, with that grin so frightfully wicked, he prepared her nipple; a cold, sterile wipe to thoroughly clean the area. The chill made her pink nipple stand to attention, flesh quivered—that and the pressure of him locked inside. Then the crunching of packets as he removed the steel forester forceps and needle from their packs. He pulled out, then thrust hard back inside, three times before plunging the needle through her erect nipple. He kept the steel there, quivering in her breast and thrust again; rinsing her pain with a touch of another pleasure. Her pussy gripped him as her entire body reacted, convulsing, to the simultaneous puncture. Chess licked his lips at the sight of the droplet of blood swelling around the needle protruding from her skin. His mouth dove onto her right nipple, licking and sucking her as she continued to ride the waves from the piercing and the cinching restraining her movement and breathing, shallow delirious breaths.

The rings were metaphorical at this point; to ensure longevity, the first metal was three matching long 14-gauge barbells. That was just history now, a resignation of pasts, diminished moments, that could be replayed with the donning of the ritual garment.

—

Jess stood tall and slender, dressed in her black longline satin corset and sheer black skirt draping to the floor, showing off her heavily inked skin beneath. With one hand on her cinched waist and the other on the countertop, she sucked air in between her teeth.

"So, tomorrow's your first Club, huh?"

"Yeah, it should be good," Alicia chirped.

"You getting a lift with Red?"

"Uh huh, going to hers for dinner and to get dressed. I

think she wants to 'sign-off' my look for the night," Alicia chuckled.

"Ha! Of course, can't have The Queen looking stupid. It's been a while since she's brought someone new in."

Alicia smiled and twirled a golden curl that had fallen by her face, then continued to polish the glass jewelry cabinet to the side of the counter. Within the cabinet were special custom pieces of silver created by a local designer and club member. Items included shackle earrings, charm bracelets with little floggers, dildos, butt plugs, cuffs and such charms, a cat-o-nine-tails pendant and corset pendants. Amongst the selections were also charms of silver toadstools. They seemed misplaced but cute and unique nonetheless. A swirly cursive handwritten sign overhead read, "Club Members Only".

"Now, when you go in, don't be shocked. You'll see things, and there can be a lot of intense noise upstairs, but it's ok. It's all just play—fully consensual play. Even when sometimes it doesn't appear to be so, trust that it is. The rules are heavily ingrained in anyone who plays at Fetters. Members don't tolerate those who dare break them."

Alicia nodded at Jessica's excitable, almost giddy warning. She knew the tall, slender woman was trying to give some sort of sisterly pep-talk.

This bitch really has no idea...

Alicia smiled and nodded, retorting, "Thanks, Jess, I'm sure I'll survive."

Jess' mouth twitched a smirk that said she thought she knew better.

"Well, I'm just saying... I remember my first time and I was pretty shocked with the things that I saw, and I was *older* than you." She cocked her fine darkened eyebrow drawing her brown eyes up and down Alicia, who was physically smaller and younger. This was Jess's thing; she liked to feel superior to others—men and women alike.

"Maybe I'm just not as easily shocked as you, Jess."

Jess scoffed, "Don't be a little bitch, I'm just trying to help you, especially if you want to keep on side with Red. She won't keep you around if you don't get past a newb night at Fetters. I mean, you're just a *girl*." She hissed the word girl through her teeth. Alicia always sensed a little jealousy in her. She never outwardly reacted though, she swallowed that down and left it to do its work eroding Jess's misplaced superiority. She thought age meant wisdom and deeper experience—what a fool.

—

ALICIA WAS INTRODUCED to the club when she was just seventeen. The Red Queen had brought her as her honoured guest. Nine years her senior—and being well imbued into kink culture personally and professionally—Red recognized the seeds of kink in young Alicia. Knowing the damage these blooming shoots could cause to a soul without the right care and attention, she brought the youngling into her home; *her* school. Her home of demure, controlled seasoning for those wicked beautiful cravings yearned for by the elite and deprived alike—so long as they could pay appropriate tribute. The Red Queen was Alicia's gateway down the rabbit hole of an entirely new world.

That particular evening was a BDSM aficionado and newb pick n mix, significant in many ways deeper than that, it was also the evening she was introduced to Chess.

Fetters was in a dark, seedy part of town, outside the city's bustle, through long stretches of unlit, neglected roads. The journey in itself was one filled with anticipation of an evening that was out-of-bounds for most; dangerous, except for those who were in the know. Hidden within an abandoned industrial estate, by a gypsy camp guarded by overzealous hounds—street lights were few, and the ones that did exist buzzed and flickered unreliably; CCTV was non-existent. Externally it was dead, but once you buzzed through the steel door with the appropriate password and dress-code inspection, life lit up with a tantalising cornucopia of delightfully fiendish fetish fancies.

—

ASIDE FROM RED, Chess was the first connection Alicia embraced in an all-encompassing manner, blending her perceived kinks with her whole self. People can be so cruel, she had learned from a young age.

When her mother met her teenage girlfriend, she was thrown out with just the clothes on her back at fifteen years old. Alicia was then ushered back, from her aunt's house, to be sat at the family table with her father for a "talk". A talk about *proper* behaviour and *normal* relationships—did you know the proper way of things is to mirror Adam and Eve?— it was never "Adam and Steve" or whatever rhymes with Eve. Such deviancy could not be tolerated. It was all well and good if it was at someone else's door, but certainly not her family's.

"No such biblical perversion in the Liddell household!"

One thing was for certain in the Liddell family, being queer was a sin entirely unatonable

Such a peculiar thing to view as a perversion, one's natural sexuality, Alicia always thought of such bigotry. It aroused such pain within her to realize she came from such backwards stock. They really had no idea.

His grin sliced through the air like a blade. More than that, the Cheshire grin sliced through the very fabric of reality, leaving a glowing impression. Its imprint remained in her mind like branding, and seemed to enjoy a game of hide and seek. It became so that Alicia began to think he was always there, hiding between the trees of her mind, watching and listening to her every thought. Sometimes she'd be overcome with something altogether odd—a foreign notion, an inappropriate need to masturbate—Alicia would wonder if Chess was pulling her strings from the inside. Other times, the thought that he could see everything turned intimately inward and that he could be as much her plaything as she was his. Trapped in wonderland together.

That was the thing that caught her the night they met in the playroom, as she simply knew it then, now referred to as The Black Forest. From the shadows, his grin, so very different to any other expression in the room of lust; power and submission. His sadism, his getting off nestled cosy in the psychological, and he liked his playmates to be able to endure the longevity not met at these clubs. Fetters was renowned on the scene, but the scene had a range and let's just say, Chess was very much at the top of high demand, veering off the spectrum altogether. Alicia knew all this without even knowing how she knew. He confused her in the most peculiar of ways that she found entirely exhilarating.

Red, who had shown Alicia the literal, and metaphorical ropes, had a quirk of *her* own. She was outwardly a curvaceous, sexually assertive, kink-confident woman. A well sought after Mistress. She was all of these things, but *she* was also *he* underneath it all; the steels and silks. There was nothing sordid about this. It just never came up—her gender was always assumed—and she let few close enough to know any different. Her *illusion* was infallible. She had never felt the desire to transition or come out as anything; Red was just Red, except when she was someone else entirely. Which we all are, at least the most interesting of folks. How frightfully boring it would be to wake up the same person as one was yesterday.

Red's favourite slave, known only as Rabbit, had no clue of his Mistress' entire identity. Of course, that was entirely the point of such a relationship; to box off portions that could be revealed entirely while leaving the others well under wraps, each in their own little compartmentalized world for safe-keeping. A lament configuration never to be "fixed" in one place.

One club night, Alicia had found herself engaged in a conversation with Rabbit, who incidentally belonged to another Mistress at that time. A devious domina by the name of Duchess, another sort of Red, one might say, but Rabbit had been out on the scene for a short while longer than Alicia, and he was a fair bit older in his years; a highly regarded Psychiatrist when his clothes were on. It is quite the thing to not really see someone anymore when their clothes are on. Alicia found this from her first few visits to the club. "The change" took a little getting used to—how she didn't recognise folks as the same as they were with their clothes off, strapped up, harnessed up, corseted up, sashaying about in latex. Folks at play were far more relaxing and trustworthy to be around; their most fragile and provocative areas exposed than when their civilian clothes were back on; instant barrier lift, and those bastards were heavy. How can anyone be trusted by the cover of day, now that she has found her way down the rabbit hole of liberation and wonder? The good doctor (Rabbit) was indeed good. Duchess didn't deserve a slave as loyal as this one was, and she abandoned him at a sensitive point in his journey. Red was his savior, his Queen. Sexually, Rabbit only had eyes for women, yet without penetration into a woman, his deepest fulfilment came from Red; a bio male, an extraordinary Queen. He didn't know, of course, but Alicia did always wonder if it would change should he know that detail. Not that he ever would, but still, she wondered upon many things and how dynamics shift so greatly by things seemingly so little. One cube of sugar can turn something delightfully sweet into something altogether sickly. How love can be found in the written word, but apply a voice, an accent, or a face and the axis shifts.

One of the warmest things about this perverse little family was the club night dinners. It was an unexpected thing to find upon what was in many respects a *nightclub*—that being a club that took place in the dark of night, a very elite special club indeed, but a nightclub nonetheless. Every month had its rhythm, sometimes there would be special guests and themes, of course, regardless of the inner fan-fair and fun-fair of this little torture garden. There was always time for tea, and at every event, this was a staple that could be counted on for the regulars—no newbs or underlings. This was top table stuff.

—

ALICIA'S first tea party was on her one-year membership anniversary, and she was, by this point, entwined with her throuple in Red and Chess. Neither were new to club tea.

On entering her first Tulgey Tea, Alicia's petticoats flared out playfully at her mid-calf, exposing a tease of skin between that and her Lilly-white lace ankle socks. Her cerulean blue dress was cut slightly above the white coats, made especially to fit her cinched form. She had been tight-lacing for some while now. Her first baptism into corseting had her hooked. Her cinched waist was topped with the dramatic curve of bosom and the sensational exaggeration of her hips. Her drag friends had to cinch and pad to get this effect. For Alicia, though, after years of waist training, it was effortless. Her body embraced the ritualistic tightening like the wanting touch of a devout lover. Though she did have to become a bit of a seamstress to accommodate her curves, when nothing off-the-rack fitted without alteration.

The walls of Tulgey Wood (as the dining room was otherwise known) were adorned with fantastical tall leafy trees of mesmerizing psychedelic swirls of colour. Mushrooms, hidden and pronounced of all shapes and sizes. To sit in the room was to be held in this fantasy wood. The world beyond fell away, or the diners fell from it, maybe both. Whichever it was, it failed to matter amongst the trees and toadstools that were endless. One could step into a wall and explore gardens of other minds, none greener—if any one was even green at all. The room was more of a forest than a box inside an old industrial building. The scents rolled through the room—floral, intense and heady. Notes of Tiger Lily, Peony, Rose, Jasmine, Lily and Freesia, among a tantalising cascade of notes. No matter how one entered the room, they were sure to leave as someone else almost entirely. With all the wonderful exchanges and explorations of power within the rooms of Fetters, this one was quite out of the ordinary. A childlike innocence danced through hearts in Tulgey Wood, a curiosity that was free to roam and question. It's where the curtains came down; the costume came off.

The perfect tea was always set on the long rectangle table, an array of colourful floral and herb teas, home baking (everyone contributed). The serving crockery consisted of a blend of clear cups, mugs, plates and teapots alongside prized Vince Ray pieces all set on an extravagant cloth of hand-sewn flowers reflecting the backdrop. As would be expected in a room hidden in a forest lavished in fungi—this too was a headliner for the meal. Sometimes it was in tarts, wraps, salads, curry—the fungi was an honoured guest, maybe more than that, maybe it was even the inhuman host to the events—it was everyone, and everything else was its dressing.

Myrick was always at the head of the table. Myrick Hatch was a curious looking fellow. He wore heavy theatrical makeup and brightly tailored whimsical clothing; he was never seen without his top hat, which, sat at a dinner table could be seen as rude in some circles, but maybe without the hat, Myrick wasn't quite himself, like some here weren't themselves once they put their outside clothes back on. It wasn't any of that that made him curious, though. There was just something in his eye. At least one always seemed to be watching something you wouldn't expect it to be, and his words would often jumble into streams of lyrical rhymes—often rhymeless—entangled with unprovoked emotion that sounded utterly bonkers. Alicia sometimes thought she simply lacked intelligence enough to understand this regal, though mad looking fellow. On some occasions, it was as if his voice could only be heard by a select few. Like when he was speaking to you, even in a large group, his words arrived directly to the desired ears. A targeting little psychedelic thunder of Myrick's lyrical observations, even if they were merely from his mind alone, which seemed to have its own intimate little dinner table within, and maybe even others within that. An infinity of guests and teas beneath his eccentric top hat.

A clock was *hung* in the tree by Myrick's left. The clock always read 2 o'clock, until it didn't, and then it was always 4 o'clock. Time in Tulgey Wood could be hours and hours, or mere minutes for less than that, which would make up an hour let alone several. But regardless, you would look at that clock, and you had either just arrived, or it was time to go, never in-between. It was peculiar, maybe, but those were the only times that mattered in Tulgey Wood, so that detail may well not have mattered at all.

"The girl, free-falling.
   Twisted and turning,
   Mind-bending,
   Keeps all running.
   Licks of golden curls,
   Wisps of curds, no whey.
   Making them dance-prance,
   Take chances to unscramble.
   While she twirls and burls,
   Untangle, unwind.
   All frightfully kind,
   Who knew whose mind is who's?
   Whispers long streams smooth,
   Grins keeping the jeering away.
   Armed guard is Red imperial.
   She's a bloodthirsty bitch,
   Crazed witch, snatch snitch.
   All untidy fables,
   From eyeless readers.
   Between thin lines;
   Cake, tea and rhymes.
   Time moved so fast,
   The words they tumbled, rumbled,

Broke through glass."

CANOPIES DANCED around the table as pots hovered above, filling cups of herb and floral teas. Cannibalism in the surrounding setting, but it seemed to be their fetish to be drunk and eaten like the devoted deviants dining around the top-table headed by the top hat. A bite here and a sip there, and the woods enveloped the party. Chess' grin dazzled as his face melted from his eyes and mouth spread high, up curled from his peaked teeth.

"Imagination is the only weapon in the war with reality."

His body melted, as if falling, receding into the woods in a mystical fog of purple-grey smoke.

Alicia's eyes followed a string of smoke that seemed to form a sort of limb and snaked itself around to Red, licking around her neck, whispering in her ear. Red's eyes rolled back. She licked her lips as the smoke rolled down her vivid red and black rose garden inked on her left arm, then seeped into the woods.

A chuckle came from over her head, Alicia looked upward to the grin which had placed itself in a moon that was a mere painting when they entered. Now, however, it appeared full and real. It was heavy, opalescent, fantastical—otherworldly and mystical; a living painting from a book of fairy tales radiating light into the room—if it was ever a room at all. There was never a man on this moon. It was the grin of a cat, the disembodied expression.

"Every adventure requires a first step...", it teased.

Who knew that the moon could nod? But it did, toward its body of smoke.

"You've been knocking at the door Alicia, it's time to come in."

A blue door creaked open within the trunk of a large tree. Its branches swayed in an unseen, unfelt breeze—inviting, the ticking of the clock stopped. Talk and laughter ceased with the opening of the door; Alicia was drawn to its magnetism like she was to a lover's calls.

Through the door, a rosebush nipped at her hands, drawing blood. A flirty bunch of larkspur, licked the wound and spun her in a dizzying circle. She danced gaily through a meadow and forest of flora and fungi dancers, purple smoke snaking through and with it musical notes; the puppet master of the forest. Within the tree, a grinning moon widened so much Alicia thought if it may split. It did—the moon cracked in half and a dazzling display of neon stardust began to rain around the forest. Hours of dance, and flora flirtation through smoke, and shards of magical neon starlight; she danced until her dainty feet ached and her bound body screamed a burning song to be unlaced. The inner fabric was chafing her suffocating skin. She found herself falling through a whirl of smoke and broken mirrors —each shard revealed images of dripping bloody roses and the almost maniacal grin of her Chess, herself bound with a lead in each hand and a cerulean collar around her pale neck, complete with her own hoop.

Alicia reached out for a shard showing a shackle from a door, the red door to their home playroom. The reflection quivered around her finger and began to pour up her arm like liquid mirror metal swallowing her. It poured into her eyes like mercury. Her head spun with scents of sex, lubricant, burning candles . She could smell moans and screams until she was reliving a fragment of a session with Red and Chess...

Red invaded Chess' freshly flogged ass with her long, eager tongue. Lapping, licking, and snogging his tight puckered hole, while Alicia sucked his shaft from the other side of their huge custom saltire with an opening for genitals. Chess quivered beneath them; a part of him wanted to beg them to stop. It was too much, his skin burned, and he felt the lingering sting of rising welts from the double flogging. Even without sight, he could feel which lash belonged to whom. Even with the soothing of hungry, warm, wet mouths double teaming his body, he wanted more; to feel how this ride played out. It was always like this, the adrenaline shot through his body, almost separating it from his soul. Chess would see himself spread out, shackled by ankle and wrist on the strong handcrafted freestanding (bolstered to the solid floor) x-cross, enslaved and worshipped. This was *heavenlyhell*. It was times like this, the role of slave and master really was muddied. Here, neither served; they each ruled and served the triumvirate, interconnected runes making a whole. Alicia seemed to look into herself, her throat filled with Chess' cock as she massaged his balls in her oiled hand. Alicia rose from her knees, pulled her white lace french knickers to the side of her, exposing pink glistening lips and backed onto the only part of him protruding from her side of the cross. As she impaled herself on his cock—with a gasp and flutter of eyes—the world collapsed in on itself, and Alicia, once again, sat at the Tulgey Wood table.

Alicia's hand was thrust inside her panties beneath the table, gasping and pulsing, entering a climax that she hadn't realized was happening; she had, for a time, been somewhere else entirely, deep in the woods far from the table. Her orgasm rolled from her clitoris, sending shockwaves tumbling through her belly, pouring heat and electricity through her legs and up to her rapidly beating heart. The blood rush took the sight from her eyes as she rode the waves of her own helter-skelter. The rapid blood coursing, and her panting, spun her head, and her body spasmed. In her mind, she returned to slamming her body hard against Chess, as Red yanked and sent electrical pulses through the chains attached to her nipple rings.

Slowly the memory and orgasm receded; oxygen began to roll through her again. Her body continued to quiver and tingle, but the tension softened, and her eyes fluttered open, back to the table where Myrick eyed her warmly.

"Oh, Alicia. My Alicia. Their Alicia. I'd recognize *you* anywhere…" His eyes spiralled and burst like fireworks; flamingo feathers fluttered in a plume of sparks floating flirty and soft. And then beneath that… he was gone, except for the hat perched perfectly by his exceptionally large bone teapot.

Rabbit was restrained on the rack, dressed in his staple white patent harness, complete with remote operated vibrating butt plug and white latex hood with lightly perforated eyes; complete with bunny ears. His body was lanky and pale; his entire body and aura radiated the pinnacle spirit of submission. A consensual wanting, almost demanding submission, but he had been trained well, and the demand had been worked out of Dr. Rabbit. He was absolutely at the mercy of his Queen and any she chose to share her slave with. Slaves such as Rabbit did not normally attend Tulgey Wood, so this was more out of the ordinary than anything else in this twisted little clubhouse of wonders.

Red circled Rabbit, in her second-skin; a black and red custom House of a Harlot corseted latex gown nipped, then poured as an elegant, sleek liquid fishtail from her voluptuous buttocks. The gown slit seductively at the front to her tight tuck hidden beneath her latex panties. Her deep claret, black-streaked hair was worn in a high beehive that seemed to pull her face upward in her classic stern domina poise. Studying her prised pawn upon the table, which was now in place of the usual long table. The kinky top tea party goers now perched on surrounding toadstools and large tree stump tables with their individual libations and mushroom favours. In truth, the entire scene looked a little mad. The hooded, cinched, rubber, PVC, leather and lace—their fiendish fetish fancy-fair perched in the most lavishly lush garden of Eden.

"Libations have danced,
    Merrily gay.
    In the wood of Tulgey,
    Below and around this closed door.
    Within a labyrinth of wonders,
    Sordid and splendid, we soar.
    Voices and whispers;
    A song and melody after.
    Rotations and ramming rhythm,
    Of pleasure and work play hardy.
    The merry ritual of introduction,
    Over benches, shackles,
    And wondrous wheels.
    Ridden with muffled squeals,
    Submitting to love's battle-rattle.
    Desire afire,
    From the sizzle of skin branded.
    Rings rang and stung,
    And bells locked in.
    Dances romances upon,
    The floor of falling stars.
    Their boxes beckoned,
    Underlings redressed and regressed,
    On wheels rolling tarmac.
    Tea-time,
    Meal-time,
    Rhyme-time,
    Simmering down time,
    Myrick's head of head ahead-time,

So very many heads and not enough hats,
Even so, it's fine for rats;
Not here, not now or even ever,
For we instead have only the Rabbit.
Our family tea;
The mad, the brutal,
The dastardly sinful,
Lustful wish-filled.
Surrounding this little ticker of time;
Late-time, early-time,
Keeper, doctor—must be reaper.
Red's precious gift;
To slave and top of all tables,
The heart's queen if one did not know,
Is the Queen of all hearts,
Tonight will show."

MYRICK EMERGED from a yellow door in a tree, rambling in song to the humming of a chorus of swaying flowers; it was nonsense and as much sense as almost anything—anything bonkers that is—and it was.

"You'll not be going back to yesterday after this tea of ours, Alicia." He wore a heart on his head that pulsed, a stream of blood soaked his hair and shoulders.

Red stopped by Rabbit's midriff and held out her elegantly manicured right hand. Chess materialised by her side—tall and dark in his pinstripe purple and black latex suit—and placed a large silver looking decorative claw upon Red's index finger. The claw extended its length by three inches.

"Alicia, my love. Come." Red held out her other hand.

Chess moved around to the opposite side of Rabbit, with the trademark wicked upward tilt of his beautiful mouth.

His eyes seemed to hover from his face, intensely fixed on Alicia, who moved into place laying her hand in Red's, whose eyes blackened. Chess reached over the obedient Rabbit for her free hand; he slid onto her finger an identical claw to that of their Queen, only, it was a perfect fit to Alicia's daintier digit.

"To many more new adventures, our Alicia." Myrick raised his bone cup, as did the rest of the tea party.

Red lapped around the table, coming to a stop by the shackled ankles of Rabbit. She slid them apart, wide, spreading him like points of a star on the moveable boards, and came up between his legs. Red ran her hands down his body; from his quivering Adam's apple down his almost concave abdomen. She drove her claw into the apex—the peak of the centre of his ribcage—blood pooled around the tip of her finger where it met his skin. Euphoria poured over her as she dragged her steel nail tip down his belly with the entire three inch point inside. Her fingertip glided down his belly as if unzipping a skin-suit, cutting through layers of his hot meat as effortless as a scalpel. The white ball-gag was firmly in place over Rabbit's hood, preventing him from screaming should he have been so inclined. With his deep devotion, and such a willing, even welcome sacrifice, it was unthinkable that he would dare, even if he could. Certainly not in front of the elite.

Chess was suddenly behind Alicia and brought her around as Red pulled back and walked her between the bleeding Rabbit's splayed legs. Red's hands crawled down Alicia's arms, enveloping her hands in her own. She pushed them into the slave's belly and pulled the wound open at either side. Blood pooled around pulsing organs, wiggling and quivering inside his abdomen, entirely on display for his Queen and the other guests. Scooping handfuls of the hot river of blood flowing through the man, Red brought their hands to Alicia's face and smeared it down her cheeks, then repeated this with her own.

"Drink," she commanded in unwavering authority.

To that, Chess dipped in a Lily flower flute and drank of Rabbit, raising the flute over his head. The tea party descended to the table—each with their own Lilies—dipped into the red river and drank. Myrick handed Red a set of rib shears. Towering over Alicia, Red sliced his skin over his ribs, her finger bobbing as it bounced off the bones beneath.

Then using the shears, she broke through Rabbit's ribcage to the left. Red then handed Myrick the instrument and yanked open the cavity, moving squelching flesh and bone to the side to reveal his still-beating heart. Chess' hands reached into the pit and cradled the organ as he fingered the vessels around it; a dance of the heart. Red moved around by Chess and, once again, Myrick appeared, this time with a different tool for cutting the arteries, urging Red to proceed to do so. Blood gushed, like a fountain spraying upwards, raining on the surrounding people. The organ frantically spasmed in Chess' hands. Dropping the tool, Red scooped the organ from his palms, raised it to her mouth and poured some blood down her throat. Chess took the organ next and drank before passing it on to Alicia. Instinctively she took it and mirrored her lovers, pouring from one of the severed heart horns, this water of his life.

"Why don't you have a little bite, Alicia." Myrick's wide yellow-green eyes looked on eagerly at her, and she found herself biting into the thick, veiny meat. Blood gushed as she tore at the flesh of this organ, which had barely stopped beating. She ground her teeth, moving her jaw from side to side, sawing the meat to tear off a piece. It was tough, but the blood was like hot metallic gravy and helped the heart slide down her throat; down its own rabbit hole.

"To Alicia, everyone!" The room erupted into a chorus of cheers and applause from Hatch's enthusiastic lead.

"Let the splosh commence!" he sang before breaking into a bizarre jig. It was like a highland fling, but less rigid, with more hip, and his body seemed to contort with extra joints; inhuman.

The party descended upon Rabbit, emptying him, turning him inside out. They rubbed liver and kidneys on their faces, threw bloodied bits back and forth and laughed like children having a cake fight. They played skipping games with his intestines, and played "guess the body part" with eyes squeezed shut and mouths wide open. The heart was Red's and, said for a bite each for Alicia and Chess, she devoured the large organ; she really was the Red Queen, their Queen of Hearts.

Play went on for what seemed like hours until it stopped. A blink away, and everyone was once again sitting around the main tea table, fully dressed and pristine as it always was....

The clock above Hatch's mad hatted head struck four o'clock, and it was never wrong with any time, even when there were none of the troublesome little digits at all, and it hid its face.

—

THE FOLLOWING DAY, Alicia awoke to a large red velvet box at the foot of her bed, tied with purple and black ribbons. Inside, swathed in black velvet, was a new longline brocade corset. The pattern, upon closer inspection, revealed a labyrinth within a chessboard. The elaborate labyrinth was only visible if the fabric was tilted, and looked at particularly closely. There was also a charm bracelet, which dangled an anatomical heart, a crescent moon fixed on its side, a ribcage, and a finger claw. A handwritten note read; *We thought our Alicia deserved a real boned corset, keeping the time-keeper close. The claw is for the next time, you can open the present. R & C*

She knew then—as she had on other days, but none so much as this one—with Myrick's voice booming madly from the table in her mind; there was no use in going back to yesterday because she was a different person from then.

SHE SAW RED

ONCE UPON A CRIME PART 1

(Red Riding Hood)
Jason Myers

"Hey, detective, you're gonna want to take a look at this."

Looking up from the steno pad that he always carried in the inside pocket of his blazer, Detective Jackson Wolfe placed his left thumb on the paper so as to not lose his place and peered off at the person calling for his attention.

"What do you have, Smineski?" Wolfe asked.

Officer Smineski thought to himself, *Twenty years in homicide and dispatch still can't decipher between a murder and an obvious suicide.* He nodded his head and pointed to a sheet of paper that was face down on the floor—nearly dismissed as trash under the bed.

"Looks like the makings of a suicide note, detective," Smineski answered.

Wolfe walked over and kneeled to inspect the sheet of

lined paper. He read it over twice before asking forensics to bag and tag it. Standing up and rubbing his temples, he could feel the onslaught of a migraine in the near future. The detective closed his eyes tight, attempting to block out the light in the room before opening them and staring directly at the victim in front of him.

—

Putting the last punctuation marks in her final farewell, Kyra set the pen on the table and read the note out loud. Content with the verbiage, she pulled her long red hair into a tight pony tail that ran down to the middle of her back. After watching a few knot tying videos on the web, Kyra had managed to form a decent one out of a long, green extension cord that she had hanging on the pegboard hooks in her two car, detached garage.

In her bedroom, she had attached one end of the electrical cord to the door knob of her walk-in closet. Having no exposed beams in her room, research had shown her that she didn't need to go the theatrical route and kick over a stool, flailing about like they do in the movies. Kyra found that she needed only attach the fixed cord to a doorknob on one side and around her throat with the other end. Once that was settled around her neck, all she would have to do is lean forward and let the world dissolve away as blood and oxygen ceased to reach her brain.

It wasn't as violent a gesture as the stool route would have been, but as she flung herself forward—still kneeling on the soft gray carpet of her bedroom—the motion from her body pushed the suicide note off of her neatly made bed and onto the floor. Kyra watched as the paper—her admission of guilt laid out in an enigmatic confession for the police to discover—floated like a feather to the carpet. The green cord slid up the nape of her neck to the back of her head as she had left just a little too much slack in the line. When it moved up the back of her neck, her hair tie was forced out as she silently suffocated. Her bright crimson locks of hair dangled in front of her face as Kyra Hood felt death's cold embrace.

—

Kyra sat cross-legged in her bedroom, replaying the night of her rampage four years ago in her mind. Four years of hiding. Four years of nightmares. Four years of her trying to deny herself the guilty pleasure she took in peeling flesh from bone and draining blood from her victims.

Her vivid recollections of the night she recorded her last murder nearly half a decade ago still raised her endorphins. Remembering all the faces and all the screams as she went through the small room that served as a break room and locker room of sorts at the bakery which she once worked at always gave her a guilty smile.

Four years prior, Kyra carefully thought to herself about the plan she had been conspiring toward since she was fired from the bakery. She knew that if she could get there fifteen minutes before the shop opened it would be her best shot at having everyone in the same area. Before every shift the workers seemed to congregate in the back office and complain about the day's upcoming work load. Kyra grew tired of the same dull conversations that her coworkers seemed to reiterate every day. It was always about the "too rich fucks" spending "too much money on pastries," or the fact that Jim, their manager, always had it out for the employees and only cared about himself. Three years of working there and Kyra was at her breaking point.

—

Detective Wolfe went back to his cubicle and began uploading pictures of that evening's findings from the digital camera he kept with him at all times. The others in the precinct frequently joked to him about upgrading his cell and ditching the obsolete technology that was his Kodak. Wolfe, in his late fifties, would always pat the dated flip phone that he carried on a belt holster and state that he didn't need a micro computer in his hands when he was in the field.

As the photos finished uploading into a folder he had spent the last four years adding files and random notes to, Jackson Wolfe clicked on the title of the folder that said *Grandma's Kitchen Massacre: 2010-Unsolved* and deleted the last word and changed it to *K. Hood: Solved*. The last picture—the one of the suicide/confession letter—finished uploading and Jackson spent several minutes reading and analyzing the words Kyra had written.

Nearly half a decade after the carnage, the wake that Kyra —Detective Wolfe was still struggling to believe that he finally had a name for the suspect that had consumed so much of his life—left behind was so substantial that he was dreading all the phone calls and paperwork that was essentially going to be his life for the next couple of days.

A migraine that started as a slight headache was approaching full throttle. Wolfe went for his go-to method of trying to stave it off by rubbing his temples.

He quietly said to himself, "Why the hell did you change your routine, Miss Hood? You were in the clear for so long. You had the perfect hiding spot and not an inkling of suspicion was on you. You had to have known that we knew your name."

Pressing the small X in the upper right corner of the screen, the picture of Kyra's letter disappeared and all Wolfe could see was his own reflection in the monitor in front of him. He contemplated on opening the document file inside of the folder but decided to shut down the system.

"There'll be plenty of time to put this to rest tomorrow, and the days to come, old timer," he said to his reflection. "Go home and get in the dark."

The detective stood up and put his jacket back on, covering the standard issue Glock 22 that rode safely in his shoulder holster. He picked up his keys off of the desk and quietly walked the hall toward the elevator.

—

KYRA NEVER RECEIVED an opportunity to advance from baker and counter girl to management. She was always overlooked. She had more seniority there than the majority of her coworkers, but when the time came for any management or shift lead jobs to be filled, her boss, Jim, never even considered her. Closing in on the day that Kyra would change everyone's lives forever, she finally got the nerve to ask him why.

"Why? Why is it that every time a chance to change positions comes up do you always ignore me like I'm not ever here, Jim?"

Looking down from his computer screen Jim rolled his blue eyes and answered, "Kyra, it's like this. You're a nice enough girl, and you do an okay job here..."

Kyra interrupted and lashed out for the first time at her boss. "An okay enough job? Did you really just fucking say that?"

Jim stood up and looked down at the overweight girl who looked as though she had been poured into the wooden chair more than someone who had just sat down in it. "Yes, Miss Hood. You do an okay enough job. You never really go above and beyond. Any chance for overtime you turn it down and give some sad-sap excuse about needing to go to your grandparent's house and help out. You don't apply yourself by doing more than just average baking. Customers don't come in here just because you are here. You don't make them feel like they are the most important people here." Jim scoffed and added, "You hardly even greet them sometimes."

Kyra shifted in the chair and it gave out a groan. "Just admit it, Jim, you don't promote me because I'm..." she paused and looked from her feet back up to her superior's eyes, "Because I look like this and not like Tiffany out there." Kyra used her thumb to point over her shoulder to the door that led to the break room where she would, in one week's time, ensue carnage that she never felt she had in her. Kyra held the tears back as hard as she could and continued to vent in frustration.

"If I was some skinny twig bitch like all the blonde twenty year olds you hire you would take me more seriously. And if you took the time to take *me* seriously then I would take the time to go above and beyond. Shit rolls downhill, Jim. You shit on me and expect me to smile and try harder. I don't work that way. And as far as helping out at my grandparents, that is my off time and I will choose to use it any damn way I want." Try as she might, the tears were now rolling down her swollen cheeks and onto her stained apron she wore overtop of a baggy sweatshirt.

Jim sighed and sat back down in his office chair behind the desk that separated them. "The way you look plays no role in whether or not you get a promotion," he lied. "Tiffany got promoted because when the spot opened up she took the initiative to come and see me and explain all the reasons why she deserved to be shift leader. What did you do when Daryl's two weeks finally ended?" Jim asked.

Kyra knew what she did but still felt that she was overlooked because she weighed close to three hundred and seventy five pounds. She knew that the day her previous shift leader had finished his last shift she had in fact called off. Another excuse to go to Grandma's house and stuff her face with treats rather than stand for eight hours and bake them for other people to enjoy. Kyra fired back a lie to her boss, keeping to the story she told him last week.

"I had to take the day off to help my grandmother. She had just come back from the glaucoma surgery that I told you about the day before. Her eyes were big and swollen and she needed help around her house."

Jim scoffed again at Kyra and said, "What big eyes she must have had. I get it. She needed help, but we were a person down already and needed your help and you weren't here. Point blank. You call off more than anyone here and I get more complaints about you and," Jim swallowed hard as the next part was sure to embarrass and upset Kyra, but he knew it needed to be said, "your hygiene or lack thereof, honestly. You don't take care of yourself and we have standards to uphold here."

Kyra grew more upset and frustrated and repeated, "Standards to uphold?"

Jim tried to stop himself from saying the next sentence, but the words flew out of his throat before he could swallow them back down. "No one wants to buy overpriced baked goods from someone who looks like they spend all their time trying samples of the food we sell."

"You son of a bitch. How dare you say that to me!" screeched Kyra.

She made an attempt to get up quickly from the wooden chair she was currently encased in but struggled for a few seconds before being able to get out of it. "I hate this job and I hate you. Fuck you, Jim."

Kyra, pure anger and frustration coursing through her, tossed the chair to the floor and stormed out of the manager's office.

—

JACKSON WOLFE WOKE up the following morning—no trace of his previous night's headache—and walked to the kitchen to turn on a coffee pot. The small digital readout on the front of the machine told him that it was just after six in the morning as he added scoops of grounds to the filter. As the pot did the work of brewing his coffee, Jackson booted up his laptop at the dining room table.

After so many years of working on the massacre at the bakery, it was muscle memory that kicked in without him really focusing on what he was doing. Wolfe was already opening up the folder with so many hours of investigative work saved to the harddrive. While it loaded, he poured his first cup of the day and sat back down to add a conclusion to the novel-length document he was constantly working on. Even though this case was in its fourth year and countless other solved cases had come and went, the murders at the bakery always seemed to take precedence.

Detective Wolfe was never one to file a case as "unsolved." The obsessive compulsion he dealt with made it extremely hard to accept any investigation as incomplete. He would say to himself, "They're either solved or they are soon to be solved. There is no such thing as an unfinished project." He watched the steam escape out of the top of his mug and prepared himself mentally to put an end to this madness that had caused him many sleepless nights and a lingering migraine almost weekly. He glanced at the keyboard and began typing.

MARCH 5, 2014
    2145 hours
    Frank and Marcy Hood residence
    Upstairs bedroom

SUSPECT KYRA ANN HOOD, 24 years of age, found strangled in apparent suicide.

IN AN OPPOSITE BEDROOM, Frank Clark Hood, 73 years of age and Marcy Ann Hood, 70 years of age, found dead on the floor. Both elder Hoods had throats sliced open. Per the coroner's report the bodies showed decomposition of death varying from seven to ten days prior. Kitchen knife found near bodies has been delivered to forensics for fingerprint identification.

. . .

SUSPECT KYRA HAD BEEN MIA for several years following multiple execution style murders of coworkers at a bakery on Venice Drive. On February 27, 2014 the national FBI automated database alerted our jurisdiction of the name Kyra Hood, matching social security number, and D.O.B. being used for a loan application at First Federal Bank. Bank location is two miles from Hood residence.

FELLOW DETECTIVES HUBERT, Naderline, Connors, and myself canvased all neighborhoods near the bank. Security footage from the night in question had given us a suspect— caucasian female, red hair, five foot three, close to four hundred pounds, no visible tattoos or scars. Coming up inconclusive for nearly a week, a neighbor in the 1700 block of suspect's street came forward with the address of someone who fit the description. Warrants granted per Judge Benson and executed at above date and time. Attached is suicide letter from suspect Kyra Hood.

AWAITING further analysis from the forensics team: knife identification, DNA from suspect to correlate to crime scene: current, and crime scene: bakery, four years prior.

END OF REPORT.
Detective J. Wolfe
3.6.14

—

Kyra walked in the back door to the bakery that, up until five days prior, had served as her place of employment. The round clock above the break room door told her it was 8:19 am. She stopped and placed the large olive drab duffle bag on the counter to the left of the back door entrance. Slowly Kyra unzipped it—the slower she went the less noise the zipper made as it revealed the contents it hid inside of its teeth.

She was thoroughly pleased with herself as she peered at her assortment of tools to get through the next few minutes. Aside from the almost ritualistic weapons—AR-15, two nine-millimeter pistols, and a sawed off twelve gauge Remington—Kyra brought with her a plethora of ammunition. She pushed the metal weapons aside and looked into the more rudimentary instruments she intended to use first.

Piled into the duffel was also a ball peen hammer, a green extension cord, a can of lighter fluid, and two road flares. The scenario had played out in her mind every night as she laid awake in her bed, mentally preparing herself for the upcoming slaughter.

She glanced at her wristwatch.

8:25.

Judging from the cars in the parking lot she walked in—having carefully planned and parked two lots away, knowing that if she needed to make a quick getaway, any further would lead to her getting winded and slow her escape—seeing everyone was at work preparing to open the doors at nine sharp. As Kyra reached into the bag and placed one Sig Sauer pistol in the holster she wore on her right hip, she placed the hammer in the intended slot in her carpenter jeans. Kyra pulled the hood of her oversized sweatshirt up, opened the door to the break room, stepped inside, closed it swiftly, and turned the lock behind her back as she guarded the only way in and out.

"What the fuck are you doing back here, Big Red?" a male worker asked her.

"You aren't supposed to be here, Kyra. Take your fat ass back to your double wide. No free samples today," a snickering girl belted out.

Her old boss, Jim, stood up and shouted out, "If you don't leave I'm calling the cops!"

Kyra unloaded the shotgun she had hidden behind her back directly into Jim's chest. She pumped the action and put another round into his face—as if in slow motion, the pellets from the end of the barrel tore into Jim's face—obliterating the astonished look on it. Her eyes never blinked, for fear of missing any of the glorious splatter. His nose took the initial brunt impact, disappearing into the crater. The force of the shot spun her ex boss around and she saw the exit wound on the back of his skull.

Screams from the other workers echoed off the concrete walls as they realized that Kyra was blocking the only exit.

"What's wrong, Robbie?" Kyra asked sarcastically. "No jokes about how I can't tie my apron today?"

Robbie sputtered a response. "I-I-I only s-s-said that st-stuff just clowning around."

Kyra smirked and said back, "What good is a clown without it's red nose?"

She brought the shotgun up and drew a bead on Robbie's face. Before he had a chance to make a move to evade her, she squeezed the trigger and Robbie dropped to his knees with a sickening crack—the spark of life having left his body before he landed.

"Fucking hell, Kyra. Enough of this!" shouted another employee. "You'll never get away with it."

Kyra turned her attention to the right side of the room

where the remaining five workers were huddled behind a table they were using as a makeshift barricade.

"And who is going to stop me?" Kyra asked, dropping the shotgun to the floor before pulling out the AR-15.

"You Tiffany?" She fired a round through the table, the pressed wood being no match for the projectile that pierced right through it, finding its home in Tiffany's thigh as she cowered. Kyra continued, "Maybe you'll stop me, Dustin?" Another shot, another hit. "Who's going to stop me?"

Kyra saw as one of the workers stood up from behind the table and said, "I am." She peered down the iron sights of the rifle and locked in on the boy she knew as Richie.

"I never made fun of you, Kyra. I never picked on you. I never so much as bothered you. Let me leave, please," Richie begged and took a step toward her and the exit she still had blocked.

Kyra lowered the end of the gun and motioned for Richie to walk out. He closed his eyes and took a long, deliberate breath before crossing the room. As he got next to Kyra he whispered, "Thank you." She stepped to the side and allowed him to pass. Just as he reached down to turn the handle and find his freedom, Kyra spun on her heels—unholstering the hammer from her jeans—cocked back and drove the round end into the top of Richie's skull.

"You never picked on me," she screamed at the body lying on the floor convulsing at her feet. "You never said a bad thing. But you also never said a nice thing or stopped these fuckers from saying whatever they wanted about me." She hoisted the hammer back up as far as her arm would go and brought it down with every ounce of force she could muster. It quickly caved in the top of his skull and killed him instantly. His body stopped quivering and blood poured from the gaping hole, trickling under the bottom of the door into the hall where the lighter fluid and flares waited.

Brushing her red hair from her face, Kyra directed her attention to the four remaining people she intended to murder. The two with gunshot wounds were writhing in pain on the floor. The final two employees, a young girl who, for the life of her, Kyra couldn't remember the name of, and another girl named Piper that was always less than courteous to her.

Kyra stalked slowly to the corner of the room where her victims were huddled and looked down at the two she had already shot. She pulled the Sig from its holster and put a round into the face of both of the bleeding people. The nameless girl and Piper both shrieked in terror as Kyra aimed the gun at them.

"No, I think that's enough loud noise for today. Both of you," she ordered, "backs against each other." The two girls did as was commanded as Kyra removed the extension cord from the bag she carried with her. Slowly and methodically, she tied the two shivering girls up. She was able to wrap them up four times around their midsections before tying their hands together across their chests. She tugged on the cord, making sure there was no possible way for them to free themselves. Content with her wrap job, Kyra stood up and walked to the door.

"Who's the fat shit again, Piper? Me? Isn't that what you said over and over? *Move, fat shit, you're in my way. Move, fat shit, you're going too slow.* Well, I'm moving now, aren't I?" Kyra asked rhetorically. "I'll see you in hell, Piper. And here is just a taste of what that entails." Kyra opened the door and grabbed the can of lighter fluid off of the floor where she had set it. The fumes filled the room as Kyra poured it over them and around the surrounding ground on which they sat.

"Smells like barbeque to me," Kyra belted out as she walked back to the door. As she reached the opened door, she turned around and lit the first flare. She tossed it across the room. As it reached Piper it lit the floor ablaze. She repeated the toss with the second flare, this one landing right in the other girl's lap, instantly engulfing both her and Piper. Kyra turned around and walked out of the break room that was filled with flames and smoke. Screams of pain and chaos were almost muted as the door was pushed shut by Kyra.

She walked out of the pastry shop's rear door, leaving her green duffel bag to burn up the evidence of the massacre she had just orchestrated. As she walked back to her car, two lots down, she pulled the red hood back off of her head and once again brushed her hair out of her face. She took one solitary glance over her shoulder as she continued her brisk walk away from the shop. Smoke was starting to billow out of the windows and a smile graced Kyra Hood's face.

—

DETECTIVE WOLFE LOOKED at the screen of his computer without really paying attention to what was on the monitor. He had a bittersweet feeling inside of him that, although he had closure in his case, it wasn't him who brought justice to those who died that morning at the bakery. Taking a long drink of coffee from the bottom of his cup, Jackson clicked out of the file he had just finished working on and opened the attachment he added at the end—Kyra's suicide note that was scratched hastily on a sheet of notebook paper.

TO WHOMEVER FINDS ME,

I am Kyra Hood. I fucked up and finally had to end this all. I knew I shouldn't have applied for a loan. I knew it would give me away. Maybe I wanted to get caught? All I know is I couldn't take living off of my grandparent's anymore. I know you have been looking for me. I know you were close. May this bring your hunt to a swift end. I couldn't take my grandmother teasing me any more than I could take those fuckers from work doing it. I'm tired of being everyone's punching bag. Every meal she would say "What big eyes you must have, all that food. Even bigger than your stomach. What a big mouth you must have, all that food you shovel into it. What big hands you must have, all that food you pile on your plate." Enough was enough. After I killed them, I couldn't bring myself to remove the bodies. The paranoia is getting the best of me. Every car that passes by is a detective coming to get me. Every phone call that goes unanswered is someone on the other end waiting for me to slip up and say *Hello*. May my death be as quick as possible and may I not feel any more pain. I'm tired of hurting—myself and others. I'm done.

Kyra

JACKSON READ it one final time and powered off the PC. Today, tomorrow, and the days that followed would be filled with more paperwork and interviews that he had to deal with. As he walked to his bedroom to shower and face the new day, he could already feel the beginnings of a headache creeping in through his temples.

Gonna be a bad one, Wolfe, he thought to himself. *Gonna be a real fucking big, bad one. I need coffee.*

The End...

5

SWINE OF ANOTHER KIND: ONCE UPON A CRIME PART 2

(Three Little Pigs)
RJ Roles

Just before the bullet entered his head, inevitably spraying the shabby carpet behind him with blood, bone, and brainmatter, Chief Hunter had one final thought.

How the fuck did this asshole get me?

—

DETECTIVE JACKSON WOLFE leaned back and popped two Excedrin, trying to stave off a migraine before it had a chance to even start, and chased it with the last dregs of coffee of his third cup that morning. His birthday was fast approaching, and with it, came official retirement.

Forty years on the force. Forty goddamn years.

Sitting forward, his hand moved the mouse, allowing the cursor to hover over an old file that he found himself revisiting from time to time.

What's the point? Case closed, old man. She's gone and you're on your way out. Forty years. Fuck.

Wolfe was finding it hard to come to terms with his impending retirement. Cases that had landed on his desk for the past couple of months felt like nothing more than busy work. A petty larceny here, an insurance fraud there. He knew he was being selfish, but was wanting to go out with one last big hoorah too much to ask?

"Hey, oops, sorry I didn't knock."

Wolfe looked to see Janine standing in the doorway of his office. "That's ok. What is it?"

"Chief Hunter wants to see you in his office," she said sheepishly.

Wolfe nodded in acknowledgement before she left. *What does that asshole want?* With a heavy sigh, he powered off his PC, stood and straightened his shirt before walking through the bullpen.

"Hey, you gonna make it, old timer?" Grant Conners asked.

"Ha, yeah. Need someone to get you a walker?" Hubert quipped.

Jackson Wolfe stopped on the spot and turned to face the jokesters.

"Very funny. And why are you all sitting here on your asses? Shouldn't you be out in the field solving a case or something?" he asked.

"Settle down, Wolfe," Naderline said as he walked over and leaned on Hubert's desk—donut in hand. "Not much going on and need to fuel up in case something does go down." He lifted the donut to emphasize his point.

Wolfe couldn't contain the bark of laughter that escaped his mouth. "Naderline, you're another donut or two away from a massive coronary. You three should be out there getting the job done."

He stared at the man as he laughed silently, causing his belly to jiggle. From his peripheral, Wolfe saw Conners and Hubert tense up from his blunt words.

"You're a funny guy, Wolfe. I sure am gonna miss your face when you're gone. But, uh, don't you have somewhere to be?" Naderline's eyes flickered to Hunter's office and back to him.

The quick glance wasn't lost on him but Wolfe agreed audibly. "Yeah, I guess I do."

He left the sad future of the police force to wallow in their pastries and knee slapping jokes. Knocking on the closed door that read Chief William Hunter, a voice from within told him to enter.

"You wanted to see me, sir?"

"Yes, come in, Wolfe. Have a seat. Oh, close that behind you."

He did so and saw Conners, Hubert, and Naderline all looking in his direction.

Fucking punks.

"I wanted to go over a few things with you. Now, as I'm sure you know, your retirement ceremony is coming up in a few months. While I know you haven't been getting any high priority assignments, I want you to know that I'm taking you out of the field," Chief Hunter said.

"What the fuck?" Wolfe blurted out before realizing it.

Chief Hunter raised his eyebrows in surprise. "I think that's the most I've seen you fired up in a long time," he said and laughed.

"Sorry, sir, but why? I'm almost finished. I don't want to be benched right at the finish line."

"Hmm, I get that. I really do. But the department can't handle any blowback from bad press or workers' comp claims."

Wolfe sat mystified by what he had just heard. "What bad press? I've never had a single write-up in my career."

Chief Hunter sat back in his chair, rolling his finger on the desk situated between them. "I know that, Wolfe. But it doesn't change anything. We're about to crack a big case and I don't need to be worrying about you out there getting killed, or making news headlines. 'Aged cop set for retirement dead after attempting to rescue cat from tree'."

Wolfe could feel the familiar ticks of a migraine coming on. "With all due respect, *sir*, I don't want to phone it in. I want to finish out my career with at least some dignity."

"You're past your prime, Wolfe. Been past. You should've retired years ago but the higher ups like you for whatever reason. No, as of now you'll take an undocumented leave. You will still be paid, but I don't want to see your face around here anymore."

Wolfe felt blood start to flush into his cheeks and closed his eyes, counting up to ten and back down to one.

"I think this is complete bullshit. Sir."

"It doesn't matter what you think, *detective*. Now get your shit, turn in your shield and gun, and get out."

Chief Hunter turned his attention to a file that had been laying on his desk and Wolfe knew the conversation was over. He rose from the chair and left the office without another word.

Back in his office, Jackson Wolfe put the few personal items he kept there in his satchel. Before leaving, he backed up all of his research and casenotes onto a portable harddrive and cleared them off of the computer. With one final look around he flipped the light switch off and shut the door.

Hubert, Conner, and Naderline stood nearby, huddled over mugs of coffee.

"Be seeing ya, Wolfe," Naderline called as Wolfe left the building.

—

Two weeks had gone by since being exiled from the precinct and Jackson Wolfe was already tired of his own company. Normally he would have work to occupy his time, but being forced into early retirement left him feeling listless.

"I have to get out of here," Wolfe said to no one and grabbed his keys.

Walking into Andy's Diner, he sat on one of the vacant stools at the counter.

"How are you this morning, sugar?"

"I'm alright, Robin. How's your son?"

Robin rolled her eyes. "Stubborn as ever, but he'll come around. If not, I'll knock him in the head with this."

She held up the coffee pot she was using to fill Wolfe's cup.

"Say no more, I don't want to be an accessory to a premeditated assault."

Robin laughed, "Same as always?"

Wolfe nodded his head. "Same as always."

"Andy, two eggs over easy and a couple of sausage patties. Rye toast, grilled."

"Thank you, dear," Wolfe said, sipping his coffee.

With his appetite satiated, Jackson Wolfe sat back and took in the ambient conversation going on around the diner. It reminded him of a stake out he had done many years ago and struck him with an idea.

I'll tune in to the police band.

It was a simple idea, but it just might be the thing he needed to occupy his mind until his official retirement.

Jackson Wolfe called for the check and thanked Robin for her hospitality. Raising a hand to Andy as he left, he walked to his car with a new purpose.

—

With his personal vehicle now outfitted with a police band radio like the one he had in his unmarked car, Wolfe took to listening to it whenever time permitted. So far he'd only followed up on a few calls that turned out to be nothing more than the typical domestic or neighbor squabble.

"Calling all units, we have a report of gunfire out on Industrial Drive."

"Dispatch, unit nine is in the area. We'll check it out."

"Copy that, unit nine."

What in the...

Wolfe recognized Conners' high-pitched, squeaky voice instantly.

There isn't anything out on Industrial Drive except some old abandoned factories. And when the fuck did Conners start going out on patrols?

Jackson Wolfe tapped his fingers on the steering wheel as he rolled everything around in his head. From his current location he estimated that it would take him fifteen minutes to get there—conservatively. Throwing the gear into drive, he headed down the road.

Wolfe flipped off the headlights when he pulled onto the old abandoned, and creeped along while looking for any signs of life. His eyes weren't what they used to be, but he trusted his instincts that had never failed him.

In the distance he saw the headlights of three cars illuminating the otherwise pitch black. Wolfe parked, grabbed the snub nose he kept in the glove compartment, and moved in closer on foot.

"Dig it deep. We don't need no kids out here partying to find her."

"That's easy for you to say, you ain't the one digging."

"Hey, who's the dumbass that only brought two shovels?"

"Yeah, yeah, yeah."

"Shut the fuck up, both of you."

Wolfe ducked back behind the building he was using as cover. Conners, Naderline, and Hubert were busy digging a hole when he found what the headlights were being used for.

"Thought I heard something," Naderline said. "Here, you take a turn," he told Conners as he struggled to hoist his bulk out of the hole.

"Fine, but this is some bullshit. Why do we always get stuck cleaning up the boss' dirty work?"

"That's how shit rolls, down hill, and you're at the very bottom, Conners. Keep diggin', I gotta take a piss."

Hubert laughed at the joke and leaned against his shovel. "I agree, Hunter should be the one out here breaking his back. He's the one that killed her in the first place."

Conners leaned back and wiped the sweat from his brow. "It's getting to be a concern, really. What is she, the fourth or fifth we've had to plant in the ground?"

"Seventh by my count," Hubert replied.

"Fuck, he don't know when to stop. If he ever goes down for it, we're in deep shit."

"That's why we get paid the big bucks. To make it all go away."

"Psh, yeah… big bucks. Fuck it, it's deep enough. Grab'er and let's get this shit over with."

Wolfe watched as Hubert finally got himself out of the makeshift grave—on his third attempt—and walked over to the trunk of the nearest car.

"Ugh, Jesus. What did he do to her?"

Conners huffed and puffed from his own struggle of getting out of the hole—even though it was only slightly over waist high, Wolfe noted—and stood looking into the trunk.

"He's sick, man. Ain't right in the head."

A sweat broke out on Wolfe's brow as all of these revelations were hitting him at once.

Hunter? These fucks? How deep does the corruption run?

The view of the girl in the truck was obscured from Wolfe. He needed to know what he was dealing with—possibly identify the victim—and needed a better vantage. Spotting a pile of rubble on the opposite side of the building, Wolfe knew he would be able to see more from there.

As he turned to move, he gasped at the sight of a shadowy figure hovering over him. Jackson Wolfe didn't see whatever hit him, but felt the reverberation throughout his skull as he fell unconscious to the ground.

"Here, come get this piece of shit and toss him in with her."

"Ho-lee-shit. What the fuck is he doing way out here?"

"Who knows, but it looks like he's going to an early retirement."

"Ready? On three. One, two, three."

Wolfe felt weightless for a second, as if he was in a dreamstate and flying amongst the clouds… and then the impact of his body landing on something softer than earth jolted him back to reality.

"Well, look who's awake," Hubert said.

Wolfe held the lump on his head and looked at his hand as it came away wet. The lighting down in the hole was too poor to tell, but he knew it was blood.

Conners and Naderline stepped up to the hole—their hulking silhouettes cast by the headlight beams—and looked down at him.

"Looks like you done stuck your nose where it don't belong. I'd love to say I'll miss ya, but that would be a lie," Naderline said before motioning to the others. "Cover'em up, and let's get the fuck outta here."

Wolfe's head felt like it had been split into two. Far worse than any migraine that he'd ever experienced. The two above him started to toss in shovelfuls of dirt with glee in their eyes.

"See ya around, pal," Conners chuckled.

Wolf held up a hand to keep dirt from hitting his face and looked beyond the two to where Naderline stood making a phone call.

"Chief, we've hit a bit of a snag here. Wolfe showed up and was spying on us while we were dealing with that *other* problem. No, how the fuck should I know how he knew we were here. It's handled now. Let's just say she's got some company for the everafter. Yeah, I'll handle that and take care of his car.."

Aside from the constant ringing in his head, the layer of dirt on top of him was now preventing him from hearing anymore of the conversation. Being a detective for as many years as he had, instinct took over telling him to remain calm and not to panic.

How the fuck do you get out of this one, Jackson?

He remained docile, slowly turning, first to his side, and

then finally facing the dead woman. The weight of the dirt pressing down on him still wasn't significant.

Fuck, I'm going to suffocate before they're done.

Wolfe kept his breath even, while also trying to keep an area around his face from dirt. Ticking off seconds in his still pounding head to what he thought were five minute increments, he would shift his body upward, hoping that his would-be burial crew didn't notice.

Not wanting to press his luck any more than he already had, Wolfe held his position, focusing on keeping his heartrate low and steady.

To him, the wait was agony.

Nine hundred seconds, that's when something clicked in his head that he never thought possible. He panicked.

I gotta get out of here. I gotta get out of this fucking hole.

The oppressiveness pushing in from all sides was too much for his mind to handle. Throughout his entire life Jackson Wolfe would've never said he suffered from claustrophobia, guess he'd never been tested in that way, but in the current situation he found himself in, he now knew his limit.

"Uggghhhh," he screeched while pushing and clawing at the dirt.

His mind lapsed in focus as his heart raced. Sweat soaked into his soiled clothes. The fight or flight mechanics he'd honed over the years as a detective were both kicked into overdrive. Wolfe's hands were bloody and raw from churning through the dirt, but the adrenaline that was pumping through his veins shielded his mind from acknowledging the pain. Every ounce of energy he could muster was aimed at preventing his premature death.

And then…

Wolfe gasped—surprised and gleeful when his fingers felt

empty air—and sucked in lungfuls of dirt, choking off the little bit of air he was managing to breathe.

Heaving and clawing, the dirt acted more like quicksand than the rich earth he was fighting against. With one hand finally free, it was a race to push away enough dirt that would allow him a breath of fresh air.

With his lungs burning, Wolfe's frenzy of digging began to slow—his muscles lacking the oxygen they needed to work.

One more. One final push. Do it.

Wolfe pushed with his legs, while using his still-buried hand in a motion akin to a swimmer. Raising his head and pulling with his hand that was free from the dirt, his face broke free from the earth, allowing him to take the sweetest breath of his life.

The three dirty cops that put him in the hole had packed the top layer of dirt down hard in an attempt to cover their tracks. With renewed resolve, Jackson Wolfe managed to work his buried arm up and worked away enough dirt to be able to hoist himself out of the hole.

Every inch of his being was covered in rich earth. After hacking up as much of the dirt as he could, Wolfe laid on his back, staring up at the night sky. Stars dotted the otherwise ebony velvet blanket.

How long? How long have I been working alongside such rancid pieces of shit?

Unsure of how long he lay there, Wolfe turned to his side and gained his feet. His entire body ached; from head to toe. He started to walk to where he had parked his car—planning to call 911—and realized that he had lost a shoe during his ascent.

Fuck.

Hobbling back to where he knew his car to be, Wolfe was both surprised, and not surprised to find it gone.

At least you're thorough enough to think of it.

Unable to brush away the dirt on his face, Wolfe removed his earth-stained shirt—surprised to find his chest hair matted with mud—and did his best to free his mouth, eyes, and ears of dirt.

His bloody hands ached as he reached into his pocket to retrieve his phone. Wolfe couldn't see it in the dark, but knew by the feel of the screen that it was busted beyond use.

Who would you call, anyway? Everyone seems to be connected.

He wrapped his hands loosely with the shirt before starting his long trek back to town.

I can't believe those fat bastards tried to kill me. Well... yeah, I can. They've always been backstabbing pieces of shit, but still... Killing a fellow cop? The shit doesn't fly with me.

The world in front of Wolfe flashed red for a split second. He'd had enough of everyone at the precinct treating him like a second class citizen. Always making a joke about his age and asking if he needed help getting around.

"Got out of that fuckin' hole, didn't I?" Wolfe said to the pavement he was walking along.

His head ached, and his shoeless foot grew more sore with every step. Wolfe's head swam with a million different thoughts until finally landing on the least likely person.

Kyra Ann Hood.

At one time, he'd been obsessed with finding the person responsible for the bakery massacre. When Wolfe was called to the scene of the woman's latest double homicide/suicide, he'd been taken aback with the amount of sympathy that he had felt for the girl. After reading over the note she'd left, Wolfe had always wondered how someone, even bullied as she had been, could reach the point of no return. Tonight, he knew exactly how she felt.

It's time to right a few wrongs in this ugly world. Starting with the three porkers that had tried to end his life.

—

Naderline had found Jackson Wolfe's car a few hundred yards from where Conners and Hubert were burying him. The old prick must've had his keys on him, but this wasn't his first rodeo. The car's engine rumbled to life after he fumbled under the dash for a few minutes.

"Just like riding a bike," Naderline said, pleased with himself.

He flicked on the dome light and was impressed.

"So that's how you knew, you sneaky little shit."

He picked up the mic and keyed it. "Dispatch, this is unit nine, that call was bogus. Nothing out here but dirt and old relics." Naderline chuckled at his own joke while waiting for a reply.

"Copy that, unit nine."

"Gonna make one final round and then call it night. You have a good one."

He tossed the mic onto the floor and pulled his phone out.

"Done yet?"

"I don't give a shit," Naderline squealed. "Hurry the fuck up and then meet me at the old quarry on Love Road."

He ended the call before Conners could reply. Shifting to drive, he made his way out to the quarry.

"What the fuck took y'all so long?" Naderline huffed thirty minutes later.

"This dumb sumbitch kept taking breaks," Conners puffed back.

Hubert's jowls hung like heavy red curtains on the sides

of his face and waggled as he fired back. "Fuck you. Both of yous. We got it done. Now what the fuck are we doing out here?"

Conners and Naderline looked at each other incredulously and shook their heads in unison.

"Tying up loose strands, you fat bastard."

"You gotta lotta room to talk, *Nad*," Hubert snapped back.

Conners stepped between them, holding his hands up. "Shut your traps and let's get this hunk of junk over the edge."

The other two men grumbled under their breath, but stepped behind Wolfe's car.

"On three. One, two, three!"

Each man hoisted their bulk against the trunk as the car started to roll forward. Conners stumbled—lost his footing—and bounced his face off of the bumper, leaving a trail of blood down the back and on the bumper as he collapsed to the ground.

Hubert guffawed at him until Naderline squealed him to keep going. The car was free rolling now and the two still behind it pushed off as it neared the edge.

"Woah, that was a helluva splash. I bet you'd make a bigger one though," Naderline jisted as he and Hubert watched the car sink into the water that filled the abandoned quarry. "Come on, I need a beer and a steak."

—

BACK IN TOWN, Wolfe weighed his options. He could call the police, but he knew the local branch wouldn't be of any use.

And who knew how far the corruption spread into the state level authorities.

That poor girl. I have to make sure she's found.

The lights of Andy's Diner illuminated the otherwise dark night. An idea struck Wolfe and he hobbled inside.

"Holy shit, are you okay?" Robin the waitress asked.

He'd forgotten what he must look like as he looked around and saw the patrons looking at him with shocked expressions.

"Yeah," Wolfe said, his voice rough and scratchy. "I need you to do me a favor. Grab me a piece of paper and something to write with."

Robin stood silent for a moment before disappearing to the back. A moment later, Andy—the owner, as well as cook —came out of the kitchen.

"Jesus, Jackson. You look like shit."

Wolfe let out a half cough, half laugh before replying. "Thanks. I've been better."

Without asking for it, Andy placed a cup in front of him and filled it with coffee. "On the house."

He closed his eyes and nodded as his hand shook while he took a sip. He opened them again when he heard Robin arriving with his requested items. "I'll need an envelope or something to put this in, if you have one."

As Wolfe was writing everything that had transpired, he finished the coffee and asked for another. Andy obliged. With no detail spared on what he knew about the location of the girl's body, and the people involved, Wolfe took the piece of paper and sealed it away.

"Is there anyone we can call for you? Maybe get you something to clean up a bit?" Andy asked.

He shook his head. "No. No one can help me with this. Take this and put it somewhere safe," he said, handing Andy the letter. "If I don't come back for this by tomorrow, see that it finds its way into the hands of the media. Newspapers, TV stations... anyone but law enforcement."

Andy took it and stared at it, his face wavering in confusion. "Okay, Jackson. I'll see it done. Hey, wait. Where are you going?"

Wolfe looked back as he left. "I've got a pig roast to attend. Thanks, Andy."

"Where's his other shoe?" Wolfe heard Andy ask as the door swung shut behind him.

—

Picking up one of the paving stones used as a walkway, Wolfe used it to knock on the door.

"Who is it?" a voice inside of the house asked.

"I-I," Wolfe cleared his throat and continued in falsetto. "I need to borrow a cup of sugar, please."

"A cup of..." Naderline opened the door, ready to tell whoever was begging to fuck off, but froze when he saw who it was.

Before being given a chance to react, Wolfe drew back with the stone and slammed it into Naderlines face, causing the man to fall with a sickening thud. Blood and broken teeth littered the floor next to the unconscious man. He stepped into the house and closed the door.

Checking Naderline's pockets, Wolfe pulled out the man's phone and sent a text to Conners and Hubert telling them there was a problem, and to get to his house asap. Tossing the phone aside, he struggled to move the bulky man into the kitchen. After hogtying and gagging him, Wolfe searched until he found exactly what he needed for the others' arrival.

Pounding on the door, Wolfe kept out of sight when Conners and Hubert busted in.

"Whoa, what the shit is going on?" Hubert asked after spotting Naderline on the floor. Wolfe came around the corner and shut the front door, racking a round into the chamber of the shotgun.

"Don't move. Hands on your heads. Now!"

The two men complied.

"Move into the kitchen and—"

"You're makin' a big mistake, pal," Conners said.

"Shut the fuck up and do what I say," Wolfe barked as he slowly followed behind. "On the floor."

After the two of them plopped down next to Naderline, Wolfe tossed a length of rope to Hubert. The man looked up and his face looked as though it'd seen a ghost.

"W-Wolfe?"

"That's right, asshole, now get to it." He waved the gun to the other man to emphasize his point.

"Wolfe? Jackson Wolfe?" Conners turned to look, the color draining out of his face. "Nah, we killed you, you can't be here?"

"File a complaint," Wolfe quipped, kicking Hubert closer to Conners. "Hurry up!"

After Conners' bonds were secured, Wolfe had Hubert lay on his stomach and place his hands behind his back—to which he struggled to do so.

"I want some answers. Who was the girl?"

His patience wore thin when no one answered so he fired a shot into a nearby countertop.

"Jesus Christ, when did you grow a pair?" Conners sneered.

With the impromptu shot still ringing in his ears, the familiar pang of a migraine started to crawl behind his eyes. Hoisting the shotgun, he brought it down hard against

Conners' head, knocking him out cold. As the unconscious man slumped to the side, Wolfe moved around and pointed the gun at Hubert.

"Who was she?" he asked as he racked the pump.

"I don't know. I DON'T KNOW!" Hubert squealed. "They don't tell me nothing. I do as told and make a little green on the side. Come on, Wolfe, you know how it is out there."

He shook his head in disgust at the now blubbering man in front of him. "No. I don't."

Wolfe realized that the shotgun must've startled Naderline awake. He reached down and removed the gag.

"I want to know who that girl was, and why you were out there burying her for Hunter."

Naderline looked up and smiled at him—blood and jagged shards of teeth peeking out from behind his busted lips.

"You don't need to know why; don't want to. There's a whole world out there that would blow you fuckin' mind if you knew the things we do," Naderline told him, spitting a glob of blood at Wolfe's shoes.

"Spare me the bullshit, Mike. I was out there cracking cases when you were sucking on your momma's titty."

"Haha, that's just it, ain't it? You never saw what was right there in front of you the whole time. Us? We're just the ones that run it now. Where do you think we learned it? Kennedy, Sinclair, Hargrove… all those old bastards were in on the take, and you never knew a goddamn thing."

"That's… that's all a lie. I knew those guys, they were good people."

Wolfe caught Naderline and Hubert locking eyes. A slick grin slid over Naderline's lips.

"How do you think they always drove those *nice* cars? Big houses. I knowed you was dumb, but I didn't know you was stupid!" Hubert's head rocked back as he laughed.

Jackson Wolfe's blood boiled—more so from besmirching the names of his old friends than the insults aimed at him—and swung the shotgun, connecting with Hubert's chest. His shoeless foot slipped, sending him to one knee. Seeing Hubert's face redden as he wheezed for breath, Wolfe lost his sense of reason and started to pummel him with his fists.

Adrenaline pumped, blocking out the pain in his already injured hands, as each fist hammered into Hubert's face. Wolfe was going full-steam until he heard Naderline's words.

"Cop killer."

Whatever it was, it was enough to give him pause. He looked at his hands, at the brutalized man lying on the floor, and then collapsed. Weak sobbs left him as he held his aching head in bloodied hands.

"It happens, Wolfe. Happens to us all. We all have someone we answer to, even you. You just have a conscience, while guys like us are just in it for the money."

"Who was she? The girl..." Wolfe asked softly.

"Her? She was nobody. Just the latest in a long line. Hunter likes to have his fun... too much fun. There's at least a handful just like her buried out there. Hey? Hey, Wolfe, look at me."

His heartbeat pounded in his ears, but he looked at Naderline anyway.

"Untie me and just leave. I'll take care of everything. No one's got to know you was here."

Naderline's voice was smooth as butter, and dripped like honey in his ears. He wanted nothing more than to leave and crawl into his bed at home. Away from the light. Away from the rot that seemed to be infesting every corner of his life.

"Come on, man. Do the right thing."

Wolfe closed his eyes as every case he'd worked in his long career flashed through his mind. Every case that had gone unsolved. Every name that he'd entered into his private folder that still cried out for justice. He remembered them all.

He opened his eyes and used the shotgun to regain his feet. As Wolfe approached the still hogtied Naderline, he saw the man's face change from hopeful optimism, to utter terror.

"Wolfe? Woooolfe? No. NO!"

—

THREE MONTHS LATER

He scratched at the hairs on his chin—still getting accustomed to the beard he now sported. He looked up the local news station and watched the latest update on an ongoing investigation.

"Police are still looking for the suspect they believe was involved in what they are referring to as domestic terrorism," the news anchor said. "On August thirteenth, first responders arrived at what can only be called an absolute disregard for the safety and well being for the community. During an interview with Fire Chief Carter, he told reporters what first went through his head after arriving on scene.

"It was a total loss. By the time we got there, there wasn't anything we could do. The house was completely leveled. As if a tornado had swept in and blown it away.

"After a thorough investigation at the scene, it was discovered that three police officers had been inside the residence when multiple propane tanks exploded. Further details are still unknown at this time. Authorities urge anyone that has seen or knows the whereabouts of Jackson Wolfe to please call them as soon as possible. We'll update you when we know more."

He saw the man he'd been waiting for over the top of his laptop exit the brothel. He quickly exited out of the browser —spotting the folder labeled "Cold Cases" in the upper right-hand corner—and closed it, slipping it into his bag. Following his target, he waited until later that night to make his move.

The hotel the man was staying at was in the less reputable part of town, but it suited his needs just fine.

"Out slumming it, eh, chief? We'll see if we can't give you that 'happy ending' you're always looking for."

Rain pelted the windshield as thunder rolled in the distance. Readying himself, he took a deep breath and left his car.

After slipping past the clerk in the lobby, it was easy enough to pick the cheap, outdated lock the hotel still used. Inside the man's room, he found him lying on the bed. He shook off the last hints of hesitation as he pulled out a .38 calibre revolver.

"Keep quiet, and put these on," he told the man. A pair of handcuffs dangled from one hand, while the other held the gun pointed at his head.

The man looked confused at first until a flash of lightning lit the room, revealing who it was.

"Wolfe? How? You're in deep fucking shi—"

The revolver whipped across the man's face, cutting off his words.

"I said *quiet*," he reiterated, tossing the cuffs onto the man's chest.

The man held his face for a moment before complying with the demands.

With his hands now bound, the man sat on the edge of the bed pleading.

"Just let me go. You're already in over your head. Every

cop for a thousand mile radius knows your face and is looking for you."

He thought about it for a moment before speaking. "I just can't allow that, chief. There is enough bad shit out there in the world rather than to allow people like you to get away with it. People that wear the badge and pretend to honor their sacred duty. Get on your knees." Wolfe waved with the gun to the spot on the floor where he wanted him.

Chief Hunter complied and kneeled on the floor. The man looked up and Wolfe was taken aback. Tears. The man had tears welling up in his eyes that were beginning to stream down his cheeks. The man that was supposed to be one of the highest ranking members on the force, who had killed countless people.

"Please? I'll give you anything… just name it," Hunter pleaded. "Just not here. Not in this fucking sty."

The sky rumbled above.

"You know, there is one thing I have to admit. I think retirement suits me just fine," Wolfe said. "And I think it's time you consider it yourself."

Hunter's cries for mercy were drowned out by a thunderclap, as was the shot from the recoiling gun.

PINOCCHIO THE WOODEN HOE
(PINOCCHIO)

Matthew A. Clarke

Once upon a time, in a land made of jellybeans and ice cream, there lived a grouchy fox and a hungry cat.

"Ugh." Pinocchio shut the television off and closed his eyes, retreating into himself as the trucker continued to ride his nose. He'd rather that than watch another fucking fairy tale.

"Say it," the bearded man howled.

"I'm a real boy," Pinocchio said, muffled beneath the hairy cheeks. He felt his nose extend another couple of inches into the tacky passage.

The trucker gave a sharp, pleasured scream, then rolled off his face and onto the bed alongside the wooden man. After a moment spent gathering his strength, the trucker pulled his oil-stained overalls on and tossed a small wad of folded notes onto the pillow. Then, with a wink, the sweaty trucker slipped out of the door. "Until next time."

Pinocchio cleaned his nose off with a baby wipe while counting the cash with his free hand. Fifty dollars. After Geppetto took his cut, he'd be left with barely enough for a single hit. He sighed, sat up, and swung his feet off the edge of the bed (where they hung a foot from the ground) and ran a splintered hand across his flaking complexion.

"I'm not a real boy," he said, shrinking his meter-long nose a fraction. "I'm not a real boy."

When it would shrink no more, Pinocchio wedged the cash into the gap between his right leg and his torso and went about fixing his black leather body harness and jockstrap over his rock-hard body.

The seventeenth floor of the aptly-named Blue Light Hotel was home to all kinds of magical creatures; you had your garden-variety gnomes in rooms one through five, goblins and gremlins in six through twelve. There were rooms for talking animals and objects, and there were rooms for mermaids and centaurs. If you could think of a magical creature, the Blue Light Hotel had it—if not, they would go out and procure one (for the right price).

Pinocchio was not working on the seventeenth floor of the Blue Light Hotel because he had been trafficked; he was turning tricks because, like many of its employees, he was hooked on smack, and it was one of the only places a drug addicted fairy tale creature could earn a quick buck. He stepped out into the UV-lit hallway—which, like the rooms, were designed to deter the workers from shooting up on the job—and eased the door shut behind him.

The sound of magical creatures getting fucked was not something he would ever get used to, although he was thankful for the muted hearing his wooden ears provided. Princess Pillowpuff—a cotton ball fairy, usually the loudest of them all—was eerily quiet tonight.

Princess Pillowpuff worked out of the room opposite

Pinocchio. The punters would usually pay well to receive a hands-free orgasm from her magic star-wand. But there were no sounds of ecstasy coming from the little door across the hall, cotton or otherwise. Pinocchio looked down the garbage-strewn hallway to the stairs at the far end, then back to Princess Pillowpuff's door. He could hear the *gnat-gnat-gnat* of faun hooves clapping together and the high-pitch squeal of Ellie the elf as she put on her best pornstar-orgasm.

But not a peep from Princess Pillowpuff.

This struck him as odd for two reasons—not only was she a connoisseur of the art of orgasm, but he'd seen her enter with four shadowy men earlier that evening. At least one of them should have been a blubbering wreck by now. Against his better judgment, Pinocchio knocked twice on the door.

The lack of response did not sit well with him. He was supposed to be giving her a ride home, and there was no way she would have left without him; they both lived across the other side of the city.

"Is everything okay in there?" he called, keeping his voice to a respectable level; if Geppetto was to catch him interfering with another worker, there'd be hell to pay.

The door was unlocked—as per protocol—so Pinocchio opened it gently and peeked inside.

Ripped pink cushions were strewn haphazardly about the fairy on the round rotating bed. An empty syringe hung limply from the crook of either arm, each surrounded by several raw pricks from failed attempts at finding a vein under her cotton-soft skin. The men he'd seen entering with her were gone.

"Pillowpuff!" Pinocchio cried, rushing to her side and shutting down the bed's motor. "Stay with me, girl." A thick foam had formed at the corners of her mouth, and lifting her eyelids showed nothing but a pair of unresponsive orbs.

Pillowpuff's pink ball gown was heavily layered, making

it impossible to tell if she was still breathing. Pinocchio hitched the white cuffs up to her shoulders, loosened the rubber straps around her arms, and eased the syringes free. He checked for a pulse and breathed a deep sigh of relief when he felt a weak thud. Weak was better than none; everyone knew that fairies were prone to magical explosions when they expired. But a fairy on heroin? He didn't want to be within a mile radius if that were to happen.

Without warning, Princess Pillowpuff projectile vomited across her right shoulder, onto the semen-stained carpet. It stank of chemicals and lemon curd.

"Wand," she muttered.

"Your wand? Where is it?" Pinocchio asked.

"Taken... they'll kill him." Princess Pillowpuff's eyes rolled into the back of her head as she tried to sit up. Her yellow skin had become so pale it was almost translucent.

"Shh. Don't try to move. I'm going to get help." A squishy cotton hand grabbed him firmly by the wrist before he could stand. Pillowpuff shook her head weakly, lifted her gown above her stomach to display a gaping knife wound.

"No time."

Pinocchio instinctively recoiled, initial relief fading fast. "Who did this to you? Was it those men I saw you with earlier?"

Pillowpuff managed to control her spluttering long enough to confirm. "They will kill... King Monstro."

King Monstro, Pinocchio thought, *of course, it would be King fucking Monstro.*

Monstro and Pinocchio had a history, to say the least. Many years before he was crowned King of Toyland, Monstro—an oversized sperm whale—had swallowed Pinocchio after mistaking him for a squid. Once he'd realized his mistake, Pinocchio had been spat out and left to drift in the middle of the Mediterranean. Sure, Monstro wasn't the whale he was back then—and they had long since buried the hatchet—but Pinocchio would be lying if he said the memory didn't sting a little.

"PINOCCHIO?"

Shit.

Geppetto must have come looking for his cut after seeing his client slip out. There was no way he could make it back across the hall without being seen sneaking from the room of the dying fairy.

"WHERE'S MY FUCKIN' MONEY?"

There was a tremendous crack as the door to his room was thrown open. He was out of time. Princess Pillowpuff's breathing was becoming increasingly labored.

"Window," she rasped.

Pinocchio ran to the bathroom and found the window already open, her attackers likely having used it to make their own escape. The warm evening air carried the stench of sun-baked garbage and rotten fish, which made him a little ashamed at himself for assuming it had been emanating from Princess Pillowpuff. Before climbing through and charging down the fire escape, he cast one last look at the cotton fairy on the bed, wishing there was something more he could do for her... but even her wand would not have been enough to save her now.

"PILLOWPUFF?" Geppetto pounded on her door.

Pinocchio ran.

—

IT WAS NOT out of the ordinary for fairy tale creatures to go missing, only to later turn up dead. Humans didn't have the respect for them as they did back in the old days (not that he could blame them, particularly after a few hundred fairy tales, they just weren't all that impressive anymore). Kids these days were more interested in new and more exciting creations such as Pokémon, Transformers, and virtual-reality gaming devices. For this reason, Pinocchio knew that he should keep his wits about him until he could make it to the car, but he couldn't stop his thoughts drifting to what could have been.

Princess Pillowpuff was Pinocchio's first crush. They had planned to one day escape the city together and travel to the jungles of Columbia (coincidentally the very same jungles in which Pillowpuff's drug addiction had begun—but that's another story), where they would murder Lord Drakon, the dragon Lord, and take control of his billion-dollar fairy-drug-mule business. But that dream had gone the way of Pillowpuff's attackers now—out the window. There was no way Pinocchio could take down a drug lord on his own, and Geppetto would turn him into a coat rack, should he ever return to the Blue Light Hotel without at least doubling what he was owed.

It was around this time—while Pinocchio was wondering if he had it in him to take a machete to Geppetto's throat and call it a day—that the sky ignited in a fiery rain of pinks and purples. Pillowpuff had choked out her final breath.

Pinocchio ran for cover beneath the awning of a nearby sex store as razor-shards of rainbow and sparkling unicorn horns rained down across the city, hammering into the sidewalk and penetrating anyone unfortunate enough to be outside. A high-pitched scream drew his attention up the street on his right, to a group of drunk, bearded men that were practically falling over one another as they ran for the awning. Most were pinned to the ground by the falling projectiles—shredded by whistling rainbow shards—but one of the men was able to avoid the worst of it and dived beneath the overhang, slamming into the brickwork to Pinocchio's left.

"Pinocchi-hoe?" The burly man groaned, using a rusted drain pipe to pull himself back to his feet. Pinocchio noticed with little interest that it was the very same man that had been riding his face not twenty minutes ago. "Whatchoo doin' out here?"

Pinocchi-hoe was Pinocchio's stage name. The toy-boy had a strict rule when it came to being recognized in public —the stage name was a no-go. Usually, he wouldn't have hesitated to extend his nose through the back of the man's eye, but given the current situation, he found he wasn't really feeling it.

"Don't fucking call me that," he said, engrossed in the neon-light twister that rose into the clouds above his ex-workplace. He tried not to think about all the fairy tale creatures that were suffering excruciating deaths at that very moment.

The trucker scratched at the chin beneath his beard with a dirt-caked hand as he looked back up the street toward his friends—now no more than sparkly, soupy chunks of meat. "I gotta get to my van. I can't die here. My wife will never live it down!"

"Where are you parked?" Pinocchio asked, knowing his own vehicle was likely to be in the same condition as the rest of those parked at street level.

"Next block over, the underground. Why? Can you get me there?"

"I have an idea, but if I help you, I'm going to need a ride to Toyland."

"Are you serious?" the trucker hissed, thrusting a hand to the star-burst skies. "We'd be lucky to make it even halfway there."

"We'll be fine." His nose grew an inch. He sighed dramatically. "Okay. It's going to be dangerous as hell. But if I don't get to Toyland within the next hour, a city-wide magical storm is going to be the least of our worries." His nose shrank.

It was enough to convince the trucker that he had inadvertently become involved in something far more significant. He tucked his erection into the waist of his pants.

"All right. What's your plan?"

Using the wad of notes tucked into Pinocchio's hip-joint, as well as a few extra bucks the trucker produced from a flimsy plastic wallet, they had been able to afford a grand total of ten Purple Penetrators from the sex store—five each—and still had enough left over for a roll of bondage tape. After spending a few minutes crafting their shields, the pair made a dash for the underground car park.

—

THE PURPLE PENETRATORS were some of the most durable toys on the market. The tagline on the packaging, *Purple Exceedingly Naughty Impenetrable System—or PENIS,* lived up to its claim; the toys were staggeringly impressive at both penetration and at being impenetrable. Pinocchio made a mental note to leave a glowing recommendation on the Fairy Tale Toys site when he had the time.

The trucker had survived long enough to get Pinocchio to the Lego arches of Toyland before a rainbow-shard pierced the windshield and split his jaw. Fortunately, the Nutcrackers had already abandoned their post long before the heavy vehicle swerved aggressively, plowing to a stop halfway into the colorful guard hut.

Pinocchio was thrown violently against the dash. Without a moment's hesitation, he picked himself up and rolled out of the vehicle as it burst into flames. He skipped through the crumbling wooden-brick hut and into the entrance of Toyland. He couldn't be sure, but looking back, it appeared as if the Penetrators were unharmed even by fire. He shuddered at the realization of how close he had come to becoming kindling, before moving deeper into the arched walkway toward the yawning golden gate at the far end.

The reason the Nutcrackers were no longer at their posts was apparent the further Pinocchio progressed. They hadn't been running from the magic storm at all—something had blasted them down the entrance hall, reducing them to wood chips. Something incredibly powerful.

"You must hurry," croaked a tinny voice.

"They're already here?!" Pinocchio ran the last few steps to the golden gate. His knees clacked hollowly against the marble floor as he dropped to them and ran a bobbled hand across the edge of the gate's big, cartoonish eyebrow.

"No time," the gate mumbled. A thin trickle of oil leaked from the corner of her mouth. "Everyone's dead."

Pinocchio felt the sap rising to the surface of his cheeks. How could they hurt a poor, defenseless gate?

"Did you get a look at them?" The question garnered no response. "Gail?"

Her golden glow dimmed, and Gail the magic gate felt cold to the touch.

Pinocchio released a woody scream.

With his place of work gone—as well as his ability to afford drugs—Pinocchio didn't have anything left to lose. He picked himself up and hurried down the steps to the jellybean-cobbled streets of Toyland. Fortunately, Toyland had been built in such a way that it was entirely covered from the prying eyes of the outside world on all sides, but there was little in the way of security, should someone wish to wreak havoc from the inside (other than the Nutcracker guards, which were proving to be about as useful as an electrified condom).

Candy cane street lamps lay broken and splintered. Storefronts were smashed, and several small fires burned within many (a twitching pair of small, pointed boots hung from the nearest). Bodies of the dead and dying littered the streets, magical creatures of all shapes and sizes rattling their death throes. Pinocchio hoped to hell there were no more fairies among the dying. He blocked out the cries for help as he passed a Care Bear with its stuffing torn from its chest and pressed onward, across the squishy floor toward the palace.

There was a time, long, long ago, when seeing a donkey would bring the sound of helicopters and explosions to Pinocchio's ears, but upon seeing the group of semi-dressed donkeys in the courtyard of the palace, he realized that the years of therapy had all been for nothing.

He doubled over and vomited a ragged pile of dry wood chips.

"I'm not afraid anymore," he told himself, over the deafening screams inside his head. He could feel the end of his nose tingling—the way it did when it was about to grow—but instead of panicking, he closed his eyes, took a measured breath, and thought about what his therapist had told him.

Being stuck as a donkey wouldn't be all that bad. A friend of mine used to take me to this little place in Mexico... Tijuana, I think it was, to watch what they call the 'donkey shows'. They all looked like they were enjoying themselves. You could even earn a few pesos for your drugs, if that's what you wanted. Wouldn't be all that different from what you're doing with your life right now.

When Pinocchio opened his eyes, he found he wasn't

afraid of being turned into a donkey anymore. He'd always wanted to be a real man, but if it came to it, surely being a *real* donkey wasn't too much of a compromise?

His nose stopped tingling. He stormed across the courtyard, weaving through the guards-turned-donkeys, and took the sugar-coated steps to the palace two at a time.

By the time he reached the Throne Room, the sound of rainbow shards thumping softly into the Play-Dough canopy over Toyland had all but petered out.

Pinocchio pushed through the intricately carved regal doors.

"I was wondering when you fuckers would show your faces again," he shouted to a broad-shouldered back.

The palace was made almost exclusively of sugar—perhaps not the most ideal building material when the King happened to be a giant talking whale that sprayed seawater with each syllable.

"Ah, Pinocchi-hoe," the Coachman said as he and at least twenty of his shadowy minions turned to face the wooden man. The Coachman, a man as tall as he was wide, wore a garishly-red button-up jacket that looked fit to burst.

Monstro stood at the back of the room on his giant fin. He had clearly been working out since the two had last met—had shed his blubber to reveal a glistening six-pack and pecs of steel—although he was a lot smaller overall than Pinocchio remembered. Monstro's dinner-plate eyes scanned the hardened sugar-brick wall for a weak spot.

"Be a good piece of wood and stay there for a minute. I'll be right with you once I've killed the whale," the Coachman sneered. He narrowed his dead eyes before turning his sweat-slicked face back toward the cowering whale. He raised Princess Pillowpuff's star-wand. Several of the shadow-men closed in on Pinocchio.

"Don't you dare," Monstro spat, giving an angry puff from his blow-hole.

The Coachman began to mumble an indecipherable incantation in an ancient tongue; a cross between Sumerian and Braille.

Pinocchio's confidence was fading fast—he was severely outnumbered. The Coachman had been wise to use the distraction of the magic storm to make his move.

"Wait a minute," Monstro spluttered, his fins raising to his sides, "I've got money. You want money, right? Or whores? A man like you could surely do with relieving a little stress! Or, or..." Monstro trailed off, realizing that nothing would stop whatever the fat man had set in motion.

The star-wand flashed emerald, and a toxic-green-spear fired straight into the chest of the cowering whale King.

Pinocchio watched as a large hole formed in the King's chest and bloomed outward in a perfect circle. Beyond several inches of blubber, sections of gleaming-white bones could be seen blackening, crumbling, to reveal a mess of organs and slush. Seconds later, the hole had grown enough to allow the sloppy mess to slide out and splash across the floor. The smell hit Pinocchio like a fist to the face.

Then, as King Monstro collapsed into his own steaming entrails, when the shadow men effortlessly pinned Pinocchio's hands behind his back, he remembered; what was the one thing he had going for him that no one else had?

"The King is dead!" the Coachman bellowed, turning to face the wooden man-boy. "Soon, the entire world will be my very own Pleasure Island!"

The star-wand began to glow once again.

Pinocchio saw the opening he'd been waiting for.

"I DON'T LIKE BIG BUTTS," he screamed, making a last-minute adjustment to the pitch of his head as his nose rocketed out of his face, extending harder and faster than it had ever done before. It was throbbing, almost sentient, and threatened to throw Pinocchio off the intended target as he struggled to control it.

The tip of his nose slid through the business end of the wand with pinpoint precision, wrenching it free from the Coachman's amorphous hand and flicking it up and out of his reach. Pinocchio jolted his head violently upward as the shadow-minions at his arms wrestled with him. The star-wand spun round and round the wooden pillar as it slid toward his face, firing off deadly smog-spears at random, leaving everyone dead but the Coachman and a handful of fleeing minions.

The star-wand made a hollow *thock!* as it collided with his face. Before he could shrink his nose and retrieve it, the Coachman was on him, tackling both him and the minions that held him to the floor.

Pinocchio felt the two shadow-minions beneath him evaporate as he clattered to the sugary ground beneath the vast bulk of the Coachman. His limbs were pinned—he could feel his left leg cracking at the knee joint but was unable to do anything as it snapped clean off.

The Coachman jiggled atop him as he laughed, reveling in the sound of splintering wood.

Pinocchio could not see anything, but his nose had thankfully threaded the gap between the fat man's armpit. He was growing short of air. Each labored breath he inhaled stank of decade-old body odor. He was only vaguely aware of his right arm as it snapped off at the shoulder joint. Just as the pressure on his head became unbearable, and the Coachman's laughter turned muted, watery, he realized he could feel his little stub of a nose grinding against his face—it too, had broken off.

Pinocchio spent his final, fading thoughts dreaming of the one thing that had been his driving force in life and how now, he would never get to experience the feeling of having a real, fleshy penis.

PLLLLLRRPPP

The doughy body atop him stiffened, raised ever-so-slightly, allowing him to draw a strangled breath. Then—

PLLLLLRRPPP

The Coachman rose at a forty-five degree angle, suspended by some unseen force. Through his sap-clouded eyes, Pinocchio could see that the man's expression was stunned at the curious, cylindrical shape that continued to extend out of his gaping mouth, the tip of which was caked in gore and a foamy, mucus substance. A choked cough rattled through the big man's body as he was lifted further into the air, but it was not until he was almost standing—straddling Pinocchio's waist—that Pinocchio saw the other end of the curious shape was connected to him.

It was his wooden penis—the solid shaft had pierced the Coachman's bowel and torn up, and through, his shapeless body, exiting out of his mouth. Pinocchio flexed, and sure enough, the dead-weight wiggled along with the skewer.

As his breathing returned to normal, and the sap began to clear from his eyes, he was able to think a little clearer. He realized that his penis could shrink at any moment—he had not been aware he could extend it, after all—and that as soon as that was to happen, the Coachman's impossible weight would be right back on top of him. Standing was out of the question; with only one arm and a leg, it would be difficult even without the additional weight on his groin. Instead, Pinocchio rocked his hips, slowly, at first, then used the building momentum to roll himself to the side and slam the Coachman to the floor alongside him.

His penis was already shrinking as he began to scoot backward, and it was not long before he was able to free himself entirely and sit upright to take in his surroundings.

King Monstro was dead, that much was for sure. The entirety of his blubber had dissolved under the toxic burn of the dark magic. All that was left was a picked-clean skeleton within a puddle of stinking guts. There were several piles of ash about the palace, which he took to be dead minions, as well as a dozen or so holes in the sugar-brick walls, through which curious bobble-eyes peeked—natives of Toyland.

Princess Pillowpuff's wand had been shattered into several pieces, much like his nose.

Despite having won, Pinocchio felt defeated. What had he really achieved? Sure, he'd killed the Coachman before he could turn the rest of the world's population into donkeys, but the King was dead, as was Pillowpuff, and his workplace had been reduced to a pile of sparkling rubble.

"Pinocchio," said a shrill, squeaky voice.

He looked up from his arm, bent awkwardly on the floor, to the fluttering mirage that hovered above him.

"Blue Fairy?" It couldn't be—he hadn't seen her for several decades. But other than the crow's feet, and the heavily-wrinkled forehead, she looked the same. Her sparkling baby-blue dress fluttered as if made of water as her wings lowered her gently to the ground.

"I'm sorry I had to dip out on you last time we met. Turns out Blue Fairies and tacos don't mix too well," she said, blushing a little.

Pinocchio hadn't forgotten. Just after promising to turn him into a real boy, the Blue Fairy had disappeared without warning. He nodded with disinterest, having grown used to living in the wooden husk of a body long ago.

"But I'm here to let you know I'm still willing to honor my initial promise. Despite what you did to poor Jiminy Cricket in my absence."

That was a memory he'd successfully scrubbed from his head.

"I was angry," Pinocchio said, "You were gone. Geppetto turned to the prostitution trade, and Jiminy got me hooked on smack."

"And I can't help but feel partially responsible for that," the Blue Fairy sighed. "If I'd turned you into a real boy back then, perhaps you could have been saved from a lifetime of hurt. But it's not too late to make up for it. After seeing what you've done here today, I'm not only going to make you real, but I'm going to bind the crown to you. Crown you King of Toyland." Several cheers came from outside the palace walls as the villagers broke into a dance.

"A real *man*," he corrected, "And, thanks, but I'm not sure I want any of that."

The little creatures outside mewed.

Pinocchio looked at his broken nose, his dislocated arm, and shattered leg.

"On second thoughts, it can't exactly get much worse, can it?"

"That's the spirit!" the Blue Fairy exclaimed. She twirled on the spot, her long shiny dress billowing around her ankles. "Now hold real still. This will only take a second."

Pinocchio did as instructed—he stood as still as possible with only one leg as the Blue Fairy raised her wand and etched the shape of a stickman into the air between them. She then drew a jagged circle around it and flicked the shape forward.

Pinocchio's vision blurred as the sparkling shape rushed at him, entered him, and sent shockwaves throughout his entire body.

The agony was immediate and intense.

Being carved out of pine, Pinocchio had never experienced real pain before—the closest he'd come was when he'd fallen asleep with a joint in his hand and woken to a slightly smoking finger. But this... this was something altogether different—a type of inexplicable agony he had never even known could be possible.

Casting a wild eye down to his pink, soft hand, one thing was for sure: he was finally a real man. But the Blue Fairy had not taken one thing into consideration when turning him—that he would be transformed as he was, sans an arm, a leg, and a nose.

He collapsed to the floor, bleeding profusely and screaming for the torture to end while the Blue Fairy fired off spells at random, panicking, calling for help. Within minutes, the surviving villagers of Toyland had filed inside to see if there was anything they could do to help the man that had saved them, but there was not.

Pinocchio was already dead.

THE END

THE VENGEFUL LITTLE MERMAID
(THE LITTLE MERMAID)

Tara Losacano

They were scared.
    Ariella's sisters hardly ever left their sea-cave home anymore, and the Mer-Village was in a panic. It has been going on for weeks now. Mermaids were going missing. Nobody knew what was happening to them and they all felt helpless as their family and friends were disappearing.

Ariella swam around the room—her beautiful red hair flowing behind her—watching her three sisters crying. The latest mermaid to go missing was their youngest sister, Bella. She'd gone out for a swim, hoping to collect shells for a necklace, and never returned. The entire village went out to search and found nothing but Bella's shell bag—swaying with the current—laying on the seafloor.

"I'm going to visit the sea witch, Ursela. She must be able to help us find Bella and the rest of the missing mermaids,"

Ariella told her sisters. They gasped, looking at her in shock.

"No, you can't! She won't help you, she's an awful, evil witch. Besides, what if something should happen to you while you're gone? What if whatever took Bella takes you too?" Alexia asked desperately.

Ariella wrapped her arms around her sister and shushed her quietly. She was the oldest sibling and having lost their mother years ago, she sometimes felt more like their surrogate mother.

"I have to. Something is taking mermaids from our village and we're all in danger. Bella may still be out there somewhere and I need to try and find her before it's too late," she explained.

After speaking to her father, who had fallen into a deep depression after Bella never returned home, Ariella said goodbye to her sisters and promised she would return. As she swam away from her home she turned back for one last glance, hoping it wouldn't be her last.

As she swam, she thought nervously of the sea witch—a huge, dark octopus woman with jet-black hair, and a horrendous tentacled body. Ariella had only seen the witch once when she accidentally came across her cave while out exploring. She caught a glimpse of the monstrous woman and flipped her muscular, scaled tail as fast as it would go to get away. She heard the sea witch cackling as she swam from the cave.

Ariella was scared to go back there, but she was desperate to find her sister and to stop the disappearances of the other mermaids. The sea witch had ways of finding things out—magical ways. Ariella just hoped she would be willing to help her. She was known to be a mean, selfish sea-woman who cared for nobody but herself and her two giant eels she kept as pets.

The current grew stronger, and Ariella slowed down as she left the borders of her village. She was nervous out in the dark waters. Not only did she need to be aware of lurking predators, but also of whatever unknown danger was taking the mermaids. She swam low to the seafloor, keeping her eyes open for any potential threats.

After a couple hours of swimming, she finally spotted the mouth of the witch's cave. A chill ran through Ariella's body as she prepared herself to approach the entrance. The cave mouth was dark, and she couldn't hear any sounds coming from within. She slowly glided her way through the opening of the cave; eyes wide. The tunnel curved to the left, its walls covered in slimy algae.

Finally, she swam into a large cavern, darkness surrounded her. Ariella shivered and felt as if the water around her had grown colder.

"And why are you in my cave, little mermaid?" a deep, throaty voice sang out.

Ariella moved in circles, trying to find the source of the voice in the darkness. Finally, a glowing orb of light came from behind her and she could see her surroundings. She spotted the sea witch.

The giant, tentacled woman sat on a throne-like structure; her eels slithered around her bulbous body. Ariella felt a chill of disgust and fear as she watched them.

"I... I'm sorry I entered your cave. But I need your help. Please?" Her voice came out weak and unsure—unlike her usual self.

Ursela let out a thunderous laugh and the mermaid winced. Doubt set in as to if this was a good idea. Then she thought of her lost sister. She was out there somewhere, terrified, or dead. With that thought, Ariella felt a rush of anger flow through her. It wasn't fair. Here in front of her was a magical witch with the power to help and she laughed at her.

The sea witch seemed to study Ariella, seeing something brewing inside her, as she went through these emotions. Ursela watched her closely; a knowing smile curved up her face.

"Now wait a minute, girl. You've yet to tell me what you need help with," the octopus woman said. Ariella looked up, stunned.

"I'd like you to tell me what is happening to the missing mermaids. My sister, she has also disappeared," Ariella explained.

The sea witch lunged forward—tentacles flowing behind her—causing Ariella to jump in fright. Ursela did not attack her, but simply swam close by and stopped in front of the lit orb. Her eels followed, staying close to the monstrous woman.

Ariella watched as Ursela placed her slick, black hands on the orb. She moved them slowly and delicately, seemingly lost in the light. Suddenly, the witch laughed.

"What? What do you see?" Ariella couldn't stop herself from moving closer to Ursela, trying to look into the orb herself. She could see nothing but the glowing light.

"They're to be food. For humans, no less." The witch let out another cackle.

The little mermaid gasped at this.

What did she mean, food? Who's 'they'?

So many questions ran through her head.

"And my sister?" Ariella dared to ask.

"Gone. Fed to the humans," Ursela answered and watched as the mermaid collapsed onto the cave floor, tears streaming down her face. The sea witch had glimpsed darkness in this mermaid and wanted to see what she would do from here.

Would she go home now to mourn her sister? Or would she seek revenge?

Ariella stopped crying and lifted herself up to face the witch. Ursela looked deep into her eyes and felt the mermaid's anger, bringing a smile to her own face.

"Tell me. Who's the one responsible for this? Who's taken the mermaids and made them into food?" Ariella finally asked.

"It doesn't matter, little fish. There is nothing you can do. This *man* will continue to pluck your kind from the ocean and swallow you up. Go home now and cry to your daddy," Ursela answered.

Ariella suddenly felt hot with rage. She hated this witch, and she hated the human who stole her sister and friends. She brimmed with fury.

"No. Tell me where I can find this *man*. I need to see who has destroyed my family and my village. I need to know what's happened to my sister."

Ursela was suddenly upon the mermaid, inches from her face. The sea witch's eyes had turned black, and Ariella suddenly found herself terrified of this octopus woman and her gaze.

Then, the witch backed away slowly. She smiled, a wicked grin full of secrets.

"Okay, little mermaid. I'll tell you where this human is," Ursela said as she swam toward the orb once again. After softly touching the glowing ball for a second time, she snapped her fingers. One of her gray, slimy eels swam up to her. Ursela leaned over and began whispering to it. Ariella watched, feeling anxious. She hadn't thought this through and was now doubting herself.

What was I thinking? What could I possibly do to stop a human man?

She would probably be killed herself. She had her sisters to take care of.

Just as she was about to say something, the witch stopped whispering and the eel swam to Ariella, waiting by her side.

"My eel, Bastian, will guide you. Follow him to the ocean's edge. When you reach the shore, you will swallow this," Ursela said as she handed Ariella a black pearl. It was small, delicate. It was smooth to the touch and, as she ran her fingers around it, she felt a sudden rush of powerful energy. It was there and then gone just as quick.

"But what will this do?" she asked the sea witch.

"You will see when it is time. It will help you to complete your journey. It is very important, so hold it close," Ursela told her.

Ariella took one last look at the ebony pearl and then tucked it into her crimson shell bra for safe keeping.

"What do you ask in exchange for helping me?" Ariella asked the witch hesitantly.

Ursela shook her head and told her she needed nothing in exchange. But the sly grin on her face told Ariella she was hiding something. Without thinking too deeply about it, she set out. The eel gave his master one last slithering rub and then swam out of the cave with Ariella.

The little mermaid felt nervous about the trip. She had told her sisters she was coming out to see the witch, but they would not be expecting her to be swimming out to shore, especially with such danger out there. But she couldn't help but feel she was not going to come to harm while on this journey to the ocean's edge. Ursela could see where this human was, and if they were going to the shore, then that meant he was not in the waters at the moment. This calmed her.

Bastian, the eel, swam steadfast. He knew exactly where

he was going. He continuously turned back, as if to make sure Ariella was still following him. She had never been this far from her village, or this close to the water's edge. Her village had very strict rules about staying away from the shore, and away from humans. Ariella knew she was doing something very dangerous but she couldn't stop thinking about her sister, Bella. The witch had said she'd become food for the humans, and she couldn't even fathom what that actually meant. Man did not fish for mermaids, because man did not know mermaids existed. But maybe that has changed.

Poor Bella.

The more Ariella thought about her sister—and all the other mermaids that lost their lives in the same way—the angrier she got. She wanted to find this human and... and what? She didn't know, but she felt she needed to see for herself. Her body vibrated with anger and hatred of this man.

The unlikely pair swam for what felt like hours. When Ariella finally risked a look around at the ocean's surface, she saw that it was now nighttime. The skies that she rarely saw were dark with bright stars shining above. Then she looked to the east and saw stars floating just above the water. No, not stars. Lights. They were very close to the humans now. Very close to the shore.

Bastian flapped his tail at her and she dove back under, following him the rest of the way. It was strange how the ocean floor grew higher and higher. The water was not as deep now. Bastian broke the surface and seemed to bemotioning her toward the land. Ariella couldn't believe she could actually see the land. It looked like sand, just like the bottom of the sea. This spot was secluded and there were no humans around; an empty beach. She could see their lights not far beyond.

Bastian flipped his tail again and dove back under the water, leaving Ariella by herself. She knew it was now time to swallow the black pearl. She had no idea what might happen. Maybe she would see the man that had killed her sister once she swallowed it. Maybe it would draw the man to her somehow. Ariella wasn't sure what would happen next, but she knew she could not leave the water, and waiting around for something to happen didn't seem like a smart idea.

The mermaid reached into her shell bra and pulled the pearl out. She once again inspected it between her fingers as she floated on the surface. Ariella could feel the soft sand brushing against her tail. The ebony sphere looked like an ordinary pearl.

Now or never, she thought, and popped the pearl into her mouth and swallowed.

At first nothing unusual happened. A few moments later, Ariella felt a tremendous cramp in her stomach. Had the witch tricked her? The cramp traveled down her gut and into her tail. It felt as if her tail was being ripped apart, and she screamed out in pain. Something was seriously wrong and Ariella suddenly felt like she could no longer swim. Her tail wasn't working properly. The pain had lessened, but how would she ever get home if she couldn't get her tail to work again?

Her mind screamed at her to flip her tail. But something deeper screamed at her to stand. Ariella didn't know that word and continued to struggle. At the last moment, she forced all of her strength into her lower half. She was shocked to find herself above the water, feeling solid. She looked down and saw that her tail was gone. In its place were human legs. Ariella—stunned—began shaking. She stumbled forward and collapsed onto the beach. She was on land, and she had legs. She couldn't believe it.

After several minutes of looking herself over, and feeling her new legs, she began practicing walking on them. It took her many tries before she was able to put her full weight on the legs and actually take a step forward. But she was determined, and she'd been given these limbs to do what she came here to do: find the man that killed her sister.

Once Ariella felt confident she could walk with her new legs, she found an old piece of cloth on the beach and tied it around her waist. She knew from stories that humans wore clothes and she knew she'd bring attention to herself if she didn't cover up. The beach was full of trash; items people had discarded. It disgusted Ariella and reminded her of her hate for humans. They didn't care about the ocean, or the creatures that lived in it. They cared only for themselves.

She worked her way toward the dunes, feeling the coarse sand between her toes. Such an odd feeling, almost pleasant. She made it to the top of the small hills and stopped, looking around in awe. There were human men and women everywhere. They moved up and down a long walkway made of wood. They all looked so different from one another. Some fat, some skinny, some dark, some light, and they all wore different clothes. It was amazing to see, but Ariella didn't feel amused, she felt contempt. These people were nothing like mermaids. They didn't have beautiful, colorful shells adorning their bodies. They didn't have shiny, powerful tails to push them through the water. They didn't have luxurious, colorful hair, strong from the salt water. They were disgusting.

She walked closer, examining the storefronts on the walkway. She didn't know which one housed the murdering man that had hurt so many mermaids. The witch didn't tell her how she would find the man. She felt frustrated and ready to lash out.

That's when she spotted it.

The sign read *Sushi: Ocean's Rarest* and next to the words there was a picture of a mermaid. These rotten humans were using her mer-people as sushi. She couldn't believe it. That's what the witch meant when she said they were being turned to food. This human was hunting her family and friends and then chopping them up and serving them as sushi. Ariella trembled with shock and rage.

She worked her way through the crowd, stepping carefully. She still felt a bit unsteady on her legs, and didn't want to fall in front of these humans. As she approached the sushi restaurant, she got a better look at the mermaid picture on the sign. It looked exactly like her sister. Bright yellow hair flowing over her shoulders. A shiny, green tail—even the orange shell bra was the same. It took everything Ariella had not to let out a tremendous scream at that very moment.

She walked to the door and saw a sign hanging there that read 'Closed. Open at 9:00pm'. She pulled on the door anyway, and surprisingly it opened. Ariella walked slowly inside. She saw tables lined up throughout the area. The lights were dimmed and she could hear noises coming from the back room. She made her way toward the sounds and stepped through an open doorway. There she saw a thin man standing in front of a giant cutting board. Ariella couldn't believe what she was seeing. Laying on the cutting board—lifeless—was her sister. She had chunks of her tail missing. There were neatly sliced pieces of meat nearby, ready for serving.

"No, no. Not open yet. You must get out. Secrets of the chef must not be seen. Out!" the man, Akihiko, yelled at her, angrily. His voice sounded funny and his eyes looked squinty and small.

Ariella felt a rush of emotion come over her. This little man—this disgusting human—was the reason her village was in such a panic. The reason her sister was lying in front of her, cut up into pieces. Her body started trembling, her breaths came in hitches. Her rage was building, and she let it. It felt good.

Ariella's eyes searched the counter top, and there, she found a large knife glinting in the light. She reached out and clutched the sharp blade in her hands. As the man watched, her eyes went dark with hatred. He wanted to run, but his pride held him in place.

"I said go! We not open, and chef's secrets must not be shared," he pleaded, then added, "Please?"

He looked around for his own knife and spotted it across the room where he'd placed it before bringing the mermaid out of the storeroom. He'd kept her alive for the last couple of days, cutting small chunks from her muscular tail, and serving it to only special customers. He needed his sushi to be fresh. Tonight, he had finally killed the mermaid and planned to butcher the rest of her tail and serve all of his customers what was left. Nothing went to waste.

It took Akihiko years to finally find the mermaid village and secretly hunt them. Since serving mermaid tail, his customers have never been happier. He had a full house every night. They would laugh when they asked Akihiko his secret, and he would always tell them it was mermaid tail. Little did they know, he was telling them the truth.

As the man held his hands up, pleading with Ariella to leave, she looked down at her sister. Her once beautiful face was gaunt and pale. Her stunning yellow hair was now thin and limp.

Poor Bella, she did not deserve this. All of the mermaids that went missing did not deserve this fate. Fed to humans like they were nothing but meat.

Ariella leaned down and kissed her sister gently on the forehead. Then, before the man could react, she lunged forward and thrust the knife deep into his side. He gasped, eyes wide with shock. She pulled the knife out and just as quickly shoved it back in. His blood began leaking from the wounds onto the floor. The man stumbled and fell to his knees.

"Please..." he whimpered.

"Please? Is that what my sister said, too? And the other mermaids you murdered? My friends, my family!" Ariella screamed at him.

He looked confused and Ariella remembered she no longer resembled a mermaid with her powerful tail now replaced with a pair of human legs.

"That's right, she was my sister. I am a mermaid, and *you* will now be the *food*." Ariella slammed the knife into the man's gut and gave it a violent twist. Akihiko coughed up blood as Ariella laughed. She found herself reveling in this man's pain. She felt alive; she felt powerful. This human deserved her worst, and she would give it to him.

While Akihiko struggled to breathe, Ariella dragged his body to the backroom. She saw the tub of water and realized that her sister had been kept here; alive this entire time. With this realization came more fury. She looked down at the man and gave him a sinister smile. He tried to beg for his life once again, but could only manage small whimpers.

Ariella straddled Akihiko—knife still in hand—and went to work. She slowly carved around his head, working her fingers underneath the thin skin, and finally removed his entire face. Underneath, she found blood and muscle.

"I wonder how tender this meat will be? Only one way to find out." She giggled as she sliced a thin piece of the man's facial muscle from his body. He was barely conscious, but still aware enough to watch as she slipped the morsel into her mouth. Ariella threw her head back in ecstasy .

"Yes, this will work. Your customers will love tonight's *new* menu." Ariella laughed as she spoke. She went to work, butchering the rest of the man's body, hoping he felt every slice of the knife.

Back in the dark cave, Ursela moved away from the glowing orb, smiling with self-satisfaction. She had been right about the little mermaid, the *vengeful* little mermaid.

8

WHAT GOES INTO THE FOREST, NEVER COMES OUT

(Goldilocks and the Three Bears)
Lance Dale

What goes into the forest, never comes out...
Ever since I've been making memories, this phrase has been hammered into my head. The forest was cursed. Stories were told of an ancient evil, which lived inside; an evil heart which was protected by three beasts. I'm not sure how anyone knew about this. No one had ever gone into the forest and lived to tell the tale. I did not question the stories, though. The bruises served as a reminder. My stepmother did not like questions, especially from me.

She sent me out to get my half-sister, Goldilocks. She was her real daughter, the one she gave a shit about. Sometimes I think she makes me do this just to punish me. She knows Goldy hates me. She does too. I'm just a reminder that my father was once happy with someone else. I don't talk about him around her. The bruises—again—remind me not to do that too.

I knew I was going to find Goldy by the forest. She was always doing things she wasn't supposed to. Sure enough, she was right there, by the edge of the forest, with her friends. I could hear them all daring each other to go inside.

"Come on, you big chicken!" Goldy was shouting at one of the other girls.

"I don't see you going in." the girl fired back at her.

"Goldy, mom wants you back home," I interrupted.

"Oh, look who it is! My brave sister. Maybe she wants to go in."

Her friends snickered and laughed.

"I don't want to play games or fight with you. I'm just doing what mom asked," I replied, staring at the ground. Maybe if I didn't make eye contact, she would go easy on me.

"She's not your mom. She's my mom," she replied with a sly grin.

"Please, I don't want us to get in trouble," I pleaded.

"You mean, you don't want to get in trouble. I can do whatever I want. I'll just tell her you were trying to get me to go into the forest. Who do you think she'll believe?"

Her friends all laughed again. I tried to keep myself composed and ignore the sting of her words. She was right. Her mom never got mad at her. It was always my fault.

"My daughter would never tell a lie!" she would yell as her hand slapped across my face. I had to try something else if I was going to get her to listen.

"Do your friends' parents know you're all out playing by the forest? It'd be a shame if someone ran and told them," I said to her. The laughter stopped.

There was an uncomfortable couple seconds of silence before one of the girls said, "Come on. We better go."

"Oh, don't listen to Jennifer. No one would believe her

anyway," Goldy replied as she stared daggers at me. I looked back at the ground.

"My mom would kill me if she knew I was here. I'm not taking a chance," the girl replied.

"We'll see you tomorrow, Goldy," the other girl said as they ran off, leaving Goldy standing all alone. Her hands balled into fists. Fifteen years old and full of rage.

"Look what you did, you dumb bitch!" Goldy screamed at me.

I ignored the name. I was used to her calling me things like that. Plus, I had won. Her friends leaving meant she had no reason to stay out here.

"Come on, Goldy, your friends are gone. You can drop the act. You don't need to look cool anymore. Let's get home."

"I'm not going anywhere with you. Mom says you're just a dumb whore like your mother," she replied.

I tried to not let the words get to me, but they hurt like a punch in the stomach. I couldn't hold it in anymore. All these years of her treating me like a piece of shit... like I didn't matter. My blood boiled. I was no longer in control. Adrenaline pumped through my veins as I stomped toward her.

"You don't know anything about my mother!"

That same fucking smile appeared on her face. My anger satisfied her.

"I know more about her than you do," she replied. "Maybe you shouldn't have kille—"

Before she could finish, my body was flying toward her. I shoved her with everything I had, sending her flying to the ground. She looked up in disbelief.

"You bitch! Mom is going to kill you when she finds out you touched me," she screamed as she started to climb back to her feet.

I didn't hesitate. I shoved her again—even harder. I was so blinded by rage that I didn't even care how close we were to the forest. She stumbled backwards and fell into the first line of trees. We both froze. The last thing I saw was her terrified face as the thorns and brambles pulled her deep inside, swallowing her whole. My sister was gone.

—

I WAS silent as I walked home. Dread filled me as I replayed the image of Goldy's fear-stricken face in my mind.

I should've just left her with her friends and taken my lumps. How could I have been so stupid?

Everything I touched turned to shit. My mother, my father, and now my sister... all gone. Maybe I was the curse. Salty tears flowed as I continued the agonizing walk home.

I didn't know what I was going to tell my stepmother. Maybe I could just make something up? I'd tell her I couldn't find Goldy. She would never believe me. Even if she did, she would be pissed that I didn't keep looking. Besides, Goldy's friends had seen me. The thoughts swirled around my head. I just wished I could go back in time and fix everything, but that was impossible. I had to tell the truth, and I deserved whatever punishment I got. I was a murderer, a cold-blooded killer.

When I reached the house, I couldn't go inside. I just sat outside with my head down. Eventually, I heard the door open, which was soon followed by the sound of footsteps. They grew louder as they got closer. I didn't look up. I buried my face in my hands.

"Jennifer, what is wrong?" her voice asked.

It almost sounded like she cared. I couldn't respond. I just stared down, trying not to cry.

"Are you fucking deaf? You look at me when I talk to you!"

I looked up at her, the well of tears overflowed and spilled down my face.

"I'm s-s-s-sorrry," I stumbled over the word.

"What the hell is the matter with you? Where's Goldy?"

I tried to tell her, but the words wouldn't come out. I just kept repeating that I was sorry. I felt a sting of pain as she slapped me across the face.

"Tell me where Goldy is, or I will make you sorry!"

"She went into the forest. It was an accident, I swear," I blurted out.

A stillness filled the air. Her voice was calm.

"No. Tell me the truth. Where is Goldy?"

"It was an accident, Mom. I swear."

"Don't call me *Mom,* you little bitch. You fucking shit," she screamed as her hand once again connected with my face. She didn't stop. I fell over on the ground as she persisted, now with her feet. They kicked and stomped in a hysteric frenzy.

"Please, stop!" I pleaded, but she kept going.

"You worthless piece of shit!" she screamed.

I started to grow numb to the pain—I deserved this. I curled up into a ball and took the blows; I didn't even see her grab the shovel. All I heard was the *woosh* through the air just before it collided with my skull, sending me into a peaceful sleep.

—

When I returned to consciousness, I tried to convince myself it was all a dream. For a second it almost seemed believable. I was home in my bed, and everything was back to normal. The throbbing in my head sliced through that fairy tale. I struggled to open my eyes, and squinted at the sunlit sky as it moved above me. It took me a second to realize that I was moving too. I could feel the wagon rolling, jolting my body as it bounced over rocks and bumps. I laid still, fighting the urge to sit up and try to run.

Where was she taking me?

"Mom?" I called out.

"You shut your fucking mouth," my stepmother replied.

I tried to sit up but she jerked the wagon to a stop, slamming me back down. I could see the trees towering above me. My stomach sank as I realized where we were.

"I need you to tell me the truth. Where is Goldy?" she asked in a voice that was almost comforting. As if none of this was happening.

"I told you the truth, Mom. Goldy went into the forest. It was an accident, I swear."

"I understand," she replied.

"You do?"

"Now you're going to bring her back."

"Wha.." I didn't get the word out before she shoved the wagon with her foot, sending me barreling into the forest. One of the wheels collided with a rock, which brought it to an abrupt stop, and catapulted me into the dark woods. The thorns enveloped me and cut away at my flesh. Vines crept around my legs and tightened, pulling me further inside. The forest floor scraped at my back. I kicked and tried to fight it, but it only made their grip tighter. I was at their mercy.

What goes into the forest, never comes out...

The thought echoed in my mind as I was pulled deeper and deeper inside. I was going to die in here.

The vines loosened and slithered away as I came to a stop. I laid on my back and stared up at the canopy of trees above me. I had no idea what to do.

Where could I go? I was in the middle of the cursed fucking forest. Even if I did make it out, my stepmother would be waiting for me. I couldn't just lay here though. I shook all that from my mind and climbed to my feet.

"Goldy is in here somewhere," I said out loud in an attempt to feel like I wasn't alone. It didn't work.

I called out her name a few times—in desperation—not expecting a response. I turned in a circle trying to find some sort of path, something that looked familiar, but there was nothing. The tall trees blotted out the sun, making it feel like night. I had no idea which direction was which. Everything looked the same; sharp and uninviting. The barbs and thorns thirsted for my blood and wanted to enclose me inside like nature's iron maiden. I had no idea what else was in here with me. I felt naked, alone, and afraid.

Suddenly, there was a sound behind me. I turned to see the thorn bushes parting. They receded back and revealed a path for me to follow. I felt a puff of air hit my cheek as a butterfly fluttered over my shoulder and down the fresh trail. Its wings glowed in a bright green, as if it were lit up. I was mesmerized by its beauty. It slowed to a stop, as if it were waiting for me to follow, which I did. Once I caught up, it continued down the path.

The path shone with a bright green hue as I continued to follow the butterfly. The trees and bushes came alive with a radiant glow, swaying back and forth in a hypnotic rhythm. The fear which filled me—only seconds ago—disappeared, and was replaced by wonder. I was entranced by the beauty which lay before me.

Maybe this place isn't cursed after all. Maybe this is my liberation.

I was lost, yet, this was the most free I had ever felt. The butterfly swooped and pirouetted as it led the way. I started skipping to catch up, unable to wipe the smile off my face. It soon turned to laughter. I was so distracted by the unfamiliar feeling of joy that I did not notice the thorns filling in the path behind me, consuming it in darkness.

Ahead, the path opened up into a clearing. The sun peeked through the last few rows of trees, beyond them was a green meadow. I could not get to it fast enough. I sprinted like I was running a race. When I got there, it wasn't exertion that took my breath away. It was stunning. The air was filled with butterflies like the one that led me here. They were all colors of the rainbow. The ground was littered with various kinds of flowers like none I had ever seen. I took a large sniff, taking in the sweet smell. Rabbits hopped through the grass. Everything seemed to dance in harmony to a thumping rhythm that was coming from a tree in the center. It was wider than our house, and the trunk seemed to extend all the way to the clouds.

As my eyes scanned upwards, I saw a cage of branches around a large wooden heart. It pulsed in and out.

The heart of the forest... The stories are true!

A sudden chill slid down my spine.

The three beasts!

They were ruthless and blood thirsty. Anything which dared approach the heart felt their wrath, and was ripped to shreds. I thought about turning around and running, but I was too entranced by its beauty. My own heart seemed to beat in rhythm with it. I walked toward it—my legs seemed to move automatically. It was like I was being pulled by some unseen force. A light appeared on the trunk and traced the outline of a door, which creaked open, beckoning me to come inside. A smell—so strong it overpowered the flowers —came from within. Something was cooking.

A meal prepared just for me? It's inviting me in.

My stomach growled in anticipation. When I started to get close, something snapped me out of the trance. There was a red handprint smeared along the door. Below it was a trail of crimson, which trailed into the tree—as if something, or someone, was dragged inside.

This is a trap. I have to get out of here.

I turned to run back the way I came. The sky—which was now in front of me—had turned black. The heart of the tree beat faster, and pounded in my head. A crack appeared in the dark clouds as a pulse of electric light shattered the earth in front of me. A cold rain shot down and assaulted the ground like wet arrows. Each drop stung my skin. I jumped as another flash hit the ground next to me and exploded with sparks. I turned back toward the tree. It was my only hope. I ran without looking back. The hair on the back of my neck raised as the lightning continued to strike behind me, chasing me forward. When I was close enough, I dove through the doorway and landed inside the tree. My body skidded to a stop on the wet wooden floor. When I jerked around and looked through the open doorway, everything was calm outside. There was no sign of the storm. The rabbits hopped around, and the butterflies once again fluttered about. I started to crawl back but was startled when the door slammed shut and trapped me inside.

—

THE SIZE of this place seemed impossible. While it looked large on the outside, the hallway in front of me seemed to go on forever. The candles on the walls shone forward and faded into darkness. It was like looking down a well, and the only direction I could go. I crept forward as quietly as possible, which seemed foolish. Whatever force was in here knew I was here. Still, I felt like I had to sneak around.

The smell I noticed outside returned and reminded me how hungry I was. My mouth watered with each step. It was so overpowering that I forgot about the danger I was in. A door appeared on my right. I thought my eyes were playing tricks on me because it seemed to just materialize out of thin air. It opened, making the smell even more powerful. I stepped through the door, unable to resist.

A large dining room stood before me. In its center was a table surrounded by four chairs. There was a sign stuck on one of which read, *For you, Jennifer.* I was shocked.

Whoever wrote this knows my name.

I had been expected. I sat down at the table. Steam rose from the bowl in front of me. It was the source of the intoxicating smell. It was some sort of porridge. I took a bite and my taste buds erupted. The flavors seemed to dance on my tongue. I had never eaten anything like it. There was a taste of honey, which complemented the savory hunks of meat that were cooked to perfection. They seemed to melt inside my mouth. I devoured the dish in what felt like seconds. I even licked the inside of the bowl to make sure that not one drop was wasted. I felt euphoric, as if I was floating in the clouds. The feeling was short-lived. A sudden sickness filled me.

What have I done? How could I be so stupid?

The room started to spin in front of me, and my stomach felt like it was being ripped apart. I got up and stumbled back to the hallway, bracing myself against the wall as I walked forward. I had to find somewhere to lay down. My eyelids grew heavy. The walls breathed in and out, and wisps of color danced before my eyes.

What goes into the forest, stays in the forest...

My inner voice sped up, slowed down, and changed pitch as it repeated the phrase in an endless loop. Another door appeared and opened. Firelight flickered into the hall. I hobbled inside and scanned the room—there were four beds. One had a sign in front of it—just like the chair in the dining room—that read, *Lay down, Jennifer. Let the sickness pass.* I did not object. I laid down and was asleep before I could pull the covers up.

—

I WAS awoken by the sound of a woman's voice. My body felt paralyzed, as if still asleep. I kept my eyes closed. I didn't want whoever was in here to know I was awake. At least... not until I knew it was safe.

"Everything has gone according to the plan," she said. "You have done well, my servants."

The phrase was followed by a chorus of inhuman growls. They sounded like nothing of this world. I closed my eyes as hard as I could, as if that would somehow make whatever was in here with me go away.

"You don't need to pretend to be asleep, Jennifer. There's nothing to fear. Welcome to your new home."

I opened my eyes, the light seemed too bright. I was sick of waking up with a throbbing in my head. I could see the silhouette of a tall woman at the foot of the bed. Behind her were three large figures.

The three beasts!

Their black shadows engulfed the room and danced on

the wall as the fireplace flickered. I had to dig deep inside to find the courage to speak.

"Please, let me leave. I want to go home." I snapped my eyes shut and tried to wish them away.

"This is your home, Jennifer. It always has been."

"How do you know my name?"

"I don't think I would forget the name of my own daughter."

"But… my mother died when I was born."

"She was not your mother. The forest is your mother. *I* am your mother. You belong to me. This is your home," she said.

I opened my eyes again, this time my vision was clear. I stared at the ancient woman who stood before me. Her eyes were as black as ink. Her white hair hung down and brushed the floor. As she smiled, I could see her sharpened teeth. It looked like the mouth of a shark.

"What's the matter? Would you prefer this?" she asked as her face shifted and changed. It was my stepmother.

"You little bitch! It's your fault your father left!" she screamed at me, then began to shift again. The wrinkles on her face disappeared and hair formed into golden curls. Goldy.

"No one likes you, Jennifer. You should just kill yourself," she said before melding back into the old woman. A witch.

"Goldy. You've seen her?" I implored as I tried to be brave.

She cackled. The beasts joined, filling the air with sickening growls. I tried not to look at them. They were like bears, but not like any I had seen before. They nearly touched the ceiling, even though they were on four legs. Patches of missing hair revealed their black leathery skin. Their round oily eyes were contrasted by their bright white teeth. They stared at me as if they were waiting to tear me apart.

"Of course we saw her, dear, she's in the other room. Why don't you get up and have a look at her?" she said with a grin. The witch pointed at an open door next to the fireplace. It seemed like it just appeared. I could've swore it wasn't there a second ago. This place was so confusing.

"Is she okay?" I felt like I already knew the answer to my question. Of course, she wasn't. Nothing here was okay.

"She is better, now, than she was before. We had to teach a lesson about trespassing. It seems she wanted all the things we had prepared for you. She did help out though... in her own way."

"It's my fault she's here. It was an accident. Please, just let me take her home," I begged.

"I'm afraid I can't do that. I know how she treats you, how *everyone* treats you. Wouldn't it feel nice to give her back what she has given you? Think of this as my gift to you."

"Please, just let me go—let *us* go."

"You're not being held prisoner. Do you see any chains? Get up and have a look at your sister," she said.

Despite how Goldy had treated me, I felt a responsibility to help her. I had to see if she was really in the room. As I stood up, the three beasts stared at me with a bubbling foam dripping from their mouths. I had to step around one of them as I approached the door, keeping my eyes on the floor, trying not to look at it.

"That's more like it, Jennifer."

I didn't respond, just continued to look down as I walked forward. It felt like there were a thousand eyes burning a hole in my back as I stood next to the fireplace and peered into the room. I was too shocked to cry out. Goldy lay on the floor—what was left of her.

Her legs and arms were missing, pools of red encircled each stump. Her pale eyes stared upward in an empty gaze. Her mouth was wide open in an eternal scream, as her swollen black tongue hung out to the side. Claw marks riddled her body in deep gashes.

"You fucking monsters!"

"Monsters? We did you a favor. *She* was the monster. Remember how she treated you? You will never be the victim of her cruelty again," the witch said.

"You murdered her," I replied.

"She deserved it. I protected you. Now, you can protect me. You drank the porridge. You sealed your fate."

I had to get out of here. I looked around the room. There was nowhere for me to go. Even if I were to make it out, where would I go? I still had to try. I scanned for any possible way to escape. I backed up and tried to get as far away from them as possible. I could feel the fire burning behind me.

"What do you think was in that porridge? Did you like the taste of your sister?" she cackled. The beasts joined in again.

I felt a sickness in my stomach and fought the urge to vomit.

"You're lying!" I shouted.

"You should be honored. You were chosen. Can you feel your body changing? It takes a little while, but soon you will be just like your new family," she said as she pointed at the beasts.

She was right, I was changing. I felt a mental and physical strength that I had never felt before.

Perhaps I can use this to my advantage.

I had to think fast.

"Come over here. It's time to get acquainted with your brothers and sister," she continued.

I turned and faced the flames in the fireplace, staring down at the burning logs.

"Quit trying to fight it. What goes into the forest, never comes out. You should know that."

I saw my chance. I reached in and grabbed one of the

burning logs, ignoring the searing pain as it scorched my hand. I cocked my arm back and faced her.

"Silly girl, you can't hurt me," she said.

I locked onto my target and released. The flaming log hissed in the air as it flew. The witch's eyes followed it as it flew over her head and landed on the bed—the sheets burst into flames. A look of disbelief flashed across her face that quickly turned to anger.

"You little bitch! Put it out!" she screamed at the beasts as they dove onto the bed and rolled over the flames.

The walls seemed to blink in and out, and suddenly, I could see outside. There was no long hallway, just an opening in the tree. Everything here was an illusion. I had to act now while the forest was distracted.

I bolted toward the door. The witch jumped in front of me. I braced for impact but went right through her like mist. I leaped through the doorway with my newfound strength. When I got outside, everything looked different than it had earlier. The beautiful meadow was now a desolate wasteland. Skeletons of all kinds littered the ground. The air filled with an ashy fog. There was a path in the trees ahead of me. I ran toward it. As I made it to the tree line, I turned to get one last look. The heart on the tree was still beating, smoke poured out of it. The witch stood in the doorway, her hateful eyes burning through me.

"What goes into the forest, never comes out!" she screamed.

Three large shapes appeared behind her. She pointed her finger at me and they thundered forward. I turned and ran, and didn't look behind me. My body was still changing as my muscles swelled and grew. I ran at an impossible speed, but I could still hear them gaining on me—I couldn't look back. I bounded down the trail like a galloping horse, my legs more powerful than ever.

Am I going to turn into one of them?

I had to get out of the forest. The only way to stop the transformation was to escape its dark magic. The beasts grew closer; right on my heels. I could smell their horrid breath as they panted behind me. The smell of rot. The last row of trees was just ahead of me. They rapidly approached. I was almost there. I could make it. A clawed hand tore at my back as I leapt forward. A trail of red mist flew in the air behind me as I burst out of the forest and somersaulted onto my back.

I made it. I won.

My victory was short-lived. A shrill voice attacked my ears.

"Where's my daughter, you fucking bitch?"

Has she just been standing here waiting for me this whole time?

I jerked in pain as she kicked me in the ribs.

"Where's Goldy?"

My brain could not comprehend what was happening. I had not just escaped the worst fate imaginable just to deal with her shit. She grabbed me by my hair and yanked me up to my feet. It should've hurt, but it didn't, she couldn't hurt me anymore. I locked eyes with her in a defiant stare.

"Fuck you," I said.

She looked at me in disbelief.

"How dare you speak to me like that. Go back in there and bring me back my daughter!"

I pushed her back.

"How dare you, you fucking bitch! Go in there right now and bring me back my fucking daughter!"

She lowered her head and charged toward me. I stepped out of the way with ease, as if she was moving in slow motion. The transformation had stopped, but I still had the strength and reflexes.

"Bring her back yourself," I said as I shoved her. She flew

backwards into the forest. The look of shock—a mirror image of Goldy—was the last thing I saw before the thorns swallowed her and pulled her inside. She was gone.

I took a deep breath, the air tasted different. Everything felt new, like I was experiencing life for the first time. I turned and headed back home.

What goes into the forest, never comes out...

This was still true. The scared little girl I used to be died in there, and the new me was prepared to live happily ever after.

The End

TONIGHT, TONIGHT

(*Rumpelstiltskin*)
Denise Hargrove

"*Tonight, tonight, my plans I make...*"

He has one of those faces, pleasant, friendly, but bland. Maybe guarded? No, definitely friendly, but reserved. He works at his daughter's school, not as a janitor, but more of a handyman. He could do everything from unclogging a toilet in the boys' room, to helping teachers hang the delicate paper chains their students had made.

"He was a lifesaver," the principal would say. "That other scoundrel left us high and dry, skipping town in the middle of the night, leaving behind a worried mother and no one to open stubborn lockers, or repaint the lines in the hallways. He was right there signing his daughter up for school, and the science teacher had just thrown down the plunger in my office, yelling that he had signed up to teach biology, not for this!" The principal usually stopped here, grabbed his tie and laughed, being his own best audience, "And that wonderful little man picked it up and offered to help, I hired him on the spot!"

The girl is also a dream, petite and pretty. The other teachers gossiped over their stale lunches, exclaiming how beautiful her mother must have been, but how she must get her delicate features and diminutive stature from her father.

He is not a large man, not someone that could pull off a tool belt and spark one of the lonely teacher's fantasies of after school activities, but he had an aura around him, something that drew them in, while keeping them away. He speaks formally, with gestures just short of bows and hat tips, he holds open doors, uses words that make the English teachers swoon, and has a handful of magic tricks that can distract even the most persistent bully.

The girl is intelligent, but doesn't flaunt it. She is kind to the other children, always helpful to the teacher, and when her father picks her up from class, she is always eager to see him. They make an adorable pair, father and daughter. No mother to be had, and no real story of where she might have gone. The others pride themselves on their restraint, as no adult has yet asked them outright what their tragic story might be. The children love him, and the girl has woven a sort of spell over her classmates and they flock to her.

Spell... where did that come from? But it is the word that fits best. They have been accepted by the community where they make their home, hopefully their final home. It has been such a long chase from where it all began...

"Tomorrow, tomorrow, the baby I take..."

The same dream over and over. It is a dream, a waking thought, a nightmare... an obsession. He has her, and it's your fault. Selfish, egotistical, insecure... pathetic. The litany of words run through her head as they have every day for years. It is a mantra that keeps her going, that keeps her from being forgiven... from forgiving herself. She doesn't deserve it and even if she finds the girl, the coveted child... her child, the one he stole... she will still recite it, for there is no forgiveness for what she has done. She rubs her face hard to stop the memories but it's too late. The scenes flash before her eyes, quick, but in brilliant detail. Her husband, brutal and unrelenting. Herself, crying in the lobby of yet another crisis center. The man... no, the devil, that ruined her life, showing up exactly when she needed a miracle. How could she have known tolerating a mad man's attempt at small talk would see her, years later zig zagging across the country, searching for her stolen daughter.

"Miss, you seem quite distraught, may I sit with you?"

She had looked up, too high, lowered her gaze, and came face to face with a pair of golden eyes, under which was a completely nondescript nose and a wide engaging smile. She felt herself relax—which was against every instinct she had honed during her short year of marriage—caught herself and stared at him.

"I'm fine."

She pulled her bag close and hunched her shoulders in the universal "leave me alone you weirdo" stance that women must master to survive. Her movements aggravate the bruises and welts hidden under her clothes and she stifles her gasps, hoping the privacy intruder would take the hint. He didn't. He sits, close but not too close, and pulls out a deck of cards. Shuffling them, he turns to her.

"Pick a card."

She does... she does? Why? Before she knows it, she has pulled the one-eyed Jack, holding it in front of her face so he can't see.

"Ah yes, that makes sense," he says, more to himself than to her, "you will want to hear what I have to offer."

She stares at the card.

Isn't he supposed to guess what it is, not offer me something?

She looks into his eyes and sees danger and salvation, though she doesn't know why.

"I can help you with your Jack, he does not treat you like the queen you are and, therefore, he must be dealt with. I will handle these unpleasantries and you will leave this clinic, keeping your unborn child intact, and will give her to me at her birth."

She laughs, quick, involuntary, but loud, right in the small man's face. He is not offended, still smiling, he has put his cards away and is smoothing his vest. She takes in his small frame, neat clothes, and pointed stare, half expecting him to pull out a pocket watch and shout, "Oh dear! Oh dear! I shall be too late!"

"Look, dude, I don't know what fairy tale you think we're in, but I am here to get my pill so I can go home and take care of this mess I'm in. I really don't need you playing fairy godmother." He chuckles at this, and it quiets her. There is something happening, she wants no part of it, although falling down a rabbit hole, or flying away on a carpet would be preferable to going home to her very own ogre.

Hell, she thinks, *I'd gladly turn myself into a frog if it meant the end to this living nightmare.*

They're calling her name; she stands and looks back at him.

"If you could help me, I'd give you anything you ask for, but no one can, I made my choices and I'll live or die with them."

She follows the nurse and hears him call after her, "My dear, it will be done."

She didn't take the pill. On her bus ride home their progression is stopped by police tape and meandering onlookers, only a block from her house. She persuades the bus driver to let her off and eyes the scene as she makes her way down the broken sidewalk. A man is being tended to by a couple of EMTs. As she watches, they shake their heads and move away from the body. The man, her man—her husband of not quite a year, who has sent her to the clinic more than a dozen times during their marriage—is looking at her with dead eyes.

The next few days are a haze of cops, friends, debt collectors and a meager funeral.

"An unfortunate accident," they whisper. "He never even looked, just stepped off the curb. What a shame, not even married a year."

She giggled to herself when no one could hear and said a silent good riddance to the bastard. Months passed and her life, for the first time, fell into a calm—almost boring—rhythm. She thrived and nested, and before she knew it, her due date arrived.

Her beautiful daughter came into the world, calmly, on a wave of her mother's blood. Her face, a replica of her mother's, but her eyes so dark—like her father's—that her mother shuddered the first time they opened.

They'll lighten, she thought, *don't baby's eyes lighten, or do they darken?*

It didn't matter, she was in love at first sight and held the baby close, not letting the staff even take her to the nursery. She was dreaming of children playing in a field when the little man arrived in her room. At first she thought he was part of the dream, that she was waking and bringing those tendrils into reality as happens when one comes out of a deep sleep. But no, he was in the stark hospital room, holding her baby. As their eyes met, her body seized, as if she had been dipped in ice water. He smiled, those golden eyes playful, but all his intentions given away in that feral grin.

"She is perfect," he said, "and I will take her now."

The mother struggled internally but could not move. The little man eyed her and came to his own internal decision.

"You shouldn't try to find us, for she is mine, fair and square," he says as he backs toward the door. "But since I would hate for you to believe you weren't given a fair deal, there is one way you can win back your daughter…"

She shakes her head to stop the memories of that horrible day. The waking coma lasted three days. The inquiry to where her daughter had gone consumed weeks. With the hospital insisting they were not at fault, and no evidence that the mother had any involvement, the authorities shrugged their shoulders and put out half-hearted attempts to locate the baby of this destitute mother. The hospital, to avoid any lawsuits, quietly paid the mother a sum of money that would have kept her quite content had she chosen to accept her fate. But fueled by the audacity of the little man, the rage at the powerlessness she was tired of feeling at the hands of men, and longing to hold her daughter again, she set out to find the child. Finding them, guessing his name, what kind of madness had she been gripped with? Seven years later and all her money spent, scouring the earth in search of the answer to his riddle and the whereabouts of the unlikely pair. All her hopes now held in a scrap of paper, worn almost illegible by the many hands it had passed through.

It was time.

"*The queen will never win the game…*"

"SHE'S GETTING CLOSE!" the voice screams in his nightmare as he bolts awake, eyes scanning the room, body crouched on the bed ready to attack or defend, whichever may be needed.

He hears the girl in the kitchen pouring cereal. She is thrilled with herself that she is becoming more independent, and he knows that to succeed this time, he must start now. The mother is coming, relentless this one, and he finally has the child that will carry on his plans. After so many years, and so many discarded children, he must get this one right. He eases back down to a human-like sitting position, relaxing, breathing, realizing the threat is close but he, and the girl, are ready. Tomorrow is her birthday and she will have absorbed everything she will ever need from those that gave her life. Tomorrow she will be his and the traditions that have waited so long will once again be celebrated.

Some have called him evil, and some have praised his generosity, while others have wept when he claimed his gift. Countless many have tried to kill him. His thoughts veer from amused to dark as centuries of encounters roll through his mind. He has only ever made a fair deal; it is not his fault that people won't admit their darkest fantasies. There are so many who would give their children to save themselves, but when faced with the reality, cannot admit that they are the cowards that agree to his terms, even subconsciously. He is a Trickster, a label he accepts, better than the 'magical helper' bullshit that those self-proclaimed historians tried to saddle him with. He is here to help only himself, he needs the children, to train and send out into the world to make more offers, more deals, and acquire more children. There is no asking why, it is what must be done for his species to survive. The wealth is in the power they have to make others submit to their will. He will succeed, or he will die. And, as is the nature of the Trickster, what is the fun if there are not high stakes for both sides? So, the game is played, the dangling of hope for those mothers that may have second thoughts, the ones that can cast aside their selfishness and give a damn about the child they promised to a stranger. No one has ever won his game.

Some have found him and their stolen child, but none have bested him. Some come too late, after their bond is broken and the child itself is now the threat. Others have read the clippings—child murders, ritual sacrifice, devil worship—and been scared away. Whatever took their child years ago is not something they want to confront, and so their weak nature takes over once again, and they abandon their pursuit. He thinks about these things in a scientific manner. The training is grueling, the children are not always suited for the gifts he can bestow, and so, if their bodies cannot accept, they must be discarded. He used to try and cover his tracks, but the ancient dark part of him that drives the twisted obsession, forcing him to repeat this ceremony over and over, brings him pleasure in leaving the failures for the world to find. Fueled by the ridiculous "Satanic Panic" of the early 80s, the discovery of a mutilated child in one town caused such a frenzy and wringing of hands that he found himself fascinated. To console himself of yet another failure, he watched the coverage and speculation of "Who is Doing This to Our Children?" knowing full well that the biggest threat to any child is their parents.

This girl is powerful.

His mood sours slightly at the remembrance of the warning screamed in his dream. And when the children are powerful, there is a stronger bond with the mother. She will come for the girl and he will be ready. He ignores the uneasiness he felt with this mother, as she dangled the carrot, with his jaunty little rhyme. He saw something in her eyes that he had never encountered; *she was not afraid, she was mad.* The girl runs into the room, interrupting his thoughts, she is eager to get to school. Tonight, there is a play and she gets to kiss a frog. He laughs with her, takes her hand, and spins her in a circle, like a father should.

The school is a buzz of activity. So many parents and volunteers come and go to help prepare for the night's festivities that no one even notices the mother as she slips into the school. She wanders the halls, looking at artwork, class lists, announcements, and photos, searching for that face so much like her own, and the one that haunts her dreams. The nostalgic smell and feel of the elementary school breaks her heart as she thinks of what might have been had she not thrown her own selfish wish out into the universe for that mad man to hear. The unbelievable journey she has taken to get here wearing on her body as she stares down the colorful hallway of childhood dreams. And then... she sees her, not in the flesh, but on a poster—an announcement for tonight's play with class photos of those in the starring roles—pasted to the colorful poster board. Her own smile, cheekbones and dimples, looking back at her. But the eyes, those dark eyes did lighten, and the mother's blood ran cold.

"Come on, we are going to be late!" A shrill voice breaks the mother's trance and she turns, spotting the devil, being pulled by a small girl toward the very door she is standing in front of. She ducks in the room and slams her back into the corner. She knows the time has come and she is ready.

He lets the girl pull him, but he proceeds warily. Something is wrong and he is not accustomed to being on defense. As they enter the room, the girl stops. She feels the same connection he does, and they turn in unison toward the corner. She is standing there, he is not surprised, he knew this one would come, and now the fun begins. With his hands on the girl's shoulders, he leans forward, amused and delighted, for the game always awoke the trickster within.

"So you've come, and what may I ask do you have to say to us?"

The mother looks at him confused, astounded, then her eyes land on the girl and her face hardens. She looks back into his eyes and his wicked grin slips as he is taken off guard by the fury he sees there.

"What do I have to say to the man who stole my daughter?" she says, stepping forward. "What do I have to say to the monster who has left a trail of murdered children in his wake?" Another step. "What do I have to say to the bastard I am going to kill?" Another step, now only a foot away from the pair. "I only have one thing to say to you..."

"For Rumpelstiltskin is my name!"

And there it is, the name, spoken aloud by a voice other than his own for the first time in years, decades, possibly a century, and he knows he is done. His fingers crook into claws and start toward his face, unable to stop them, though he tries in vain. The girl falls to the floor as his body begins to seize. His fingers grasp at his face, snaring the pockets under his eyes and begin pulling as Rumpelstiltskin begins to scream. The mother is mesmerized. The little man, now the demonic creature of her worst nightmares, is pulling himself apart in front of her very eyes. She watches as his skin splits, revealing white bone and red muscle. His fingers reach inside his jaw to pull apart his very bones. The cracking and splitting and howling are too much to bear and she stumbles back, forgetting the girl, forgetting everything. As she turns to scream, to retch, to run, she remembers why she came, why she did this; her daughter. She turns back to the carnage, Rumpel's hands, now demons of their own, still clawing and ripping through the little man's body, seemingly determined to grind him to nothing. The viscera spread over the desks, dripping blood and gore down, and underneath, peering out with her golden eyes, is the prize. The mother swoops down to grab the girl and rescue her, the thoughts of her own heroism already ringing in her head. She has won the game and her own salvation, righted the wrong that she selfishly committed. As she turns to run the woman feels it on her face, breath, as the child opens her mouth. She turns to look at her daughter, to hear what the girl wants to say, and is met with teeth, teeth no little girl should ever possess.

It was a nightmare scene, growing more gruesome with each retelling. The officer carried the girl to a waiting squad car, where an ill-equipped social worker stood terrified. Buckled in, the woman used a tissue to try and wipe some of the blood from the girl's face, wondering what in the hell she was going to do with her next. She leaned back to take in the scene in front of the school. The flashing lights, gathering crowd, screams still punctuating the night as the poor teacher who stumbled upon the scene grappled with the vision that would never leave her mind. The rattled woman surveyed the chaos in silence, yet heard something; whispering.

"What is it, sweetie?" She leaned close, breathing through her mouth to avoid the smell of blood but only gaining a coppery tang on her tongue. "You're safe now."

The girl never raised her eyes, never moved, the only evidence she was speaking were the golden strands of hair waving away from her mouth as she whispered, *"Tonight, tonight, my plans I make..."*

The End...

IT'S NO FAIRY TALE OUT THERE
(FAIRY TALE MASH-UP)

Kevin J. Kennedy

Once upon a time... Nah, just kidding. It's not that kind of story. It's way more gangster. Is it a fairy tale? Yes. Is it a typical fairy tale? Well, kinda. When I think of fairy tales, I think of certain things a story must have. Generally, there is a wicked witch, or an ice queen. An evil corrupt sheriff, or a horrible old man, or woman, who steals and eats children. You know, your typical bad guy. If you have a bad guy, you, of course, need a good guy. That's pretty basic. You then add some weirdly wonderful characters, and they need a mission that will often include a journey.

You with me so far? Yeh, of course you are. You wouldn't be reading a fairy tale book otherwise. This particular fairy tale starts at the end of most of those journeys. This is a story about where all the lost characters end up. The journeys that didn't come to such a happy ending. The ones that were either too sorrowful to tell, or maybe the end of the story you know was changed a long time ago to protect the precious little kiddies. Either way, our journey will take us through the largest enchanted woods in existence. Larger than any you have read about before. Parts of the woods are covered, and good magic, while other sections are cloaked in dark magic. Some parts are just regular old woods, but the one thing I can tell you is this, no one who has entered the woods has ever left.

The enchanted woods I talk of has appeared in many tales. You will have read about it. People have mentioned it in different stories. You have likely even read different descriptions, or heard it appears in different sections of the world, or even different worlds. No one really knows. That's how magic works, isn't it? I cannot take you there. I cannot go there myself. No one can leave, but I have seen. I have travelled there of spirit, but not of body. I have a story to tell. I have answers to lost riddles. I have knowledge that no one else has, at least, not outside of the woods. We don't have much time. I'll talk for as long as I can, but I must leave my body again and travel back to the woods. I am not stuck there, but they call to me. I find it harder to stay away.

As the crystal ball clears, and the old wizard nods off. I stare into the ball as the woods come into sight, sweeping toward the trees like a hawk diving at its prey.

—

"Listen, you little cunt! I know you are fucking lying. Your nose grows every time you do. How thick are you?"

Pinocchio chaps at his own head.

"Pretty thick," he answered.

The three little pigs are having none of it. Elmer turned to Willie.

"Can you believe this little prick? How many times have we warned him?"

"Far too many. He doesn't listen," Willie replied.

Jiggs smashed Pinocchio upside the head with an open palm.

"Argh, I got a splinter off the little shit eater."

"Fuck it. I've had enough of this. Where is that woodchipper?" Willie asked.

"It's in the barn," Elmer answered. "I thought we were going to set him on fire though. It's freezing here at night. We could get heat off him."

"He isn't wrong," Jiggs agreed.

"If we light a fire, every psycho in these woods is going to come looking for us. We will be bacon sandwiches before Elmer has time to roll a spliff," Willie told them.

The pigs never used the word joint for a marijuana cigarette. Joint was a bad word if you were a pig. It didn't matter how tough they were, it sent chills down their spines.

"So, we just woodchip his ass? Seems like a waste, although I do see your point. It means our money is gone though."

Pinocchio was a massive coke head. He had the nose for it, and if he told a few lies, he needed to sniff all the more. He was always lying, trying to get drugs for free, or avoiding paying a dealer, or even just trying to get his Nat King Cole. He was fond of the ladies and, while a few wanted to ride his nose here and there, the vast majority just thought he was a big-nosed prick who should just fuck off. His various shortcomings—or long comings—had put him in the debt of the three little pigs, but it had gotten to the stage where he had one warning too many with no way out of the hole he had dug. He knew to say nothing as anything he did say would only make things worse.

"Right. Fuck it. I'm bored. Let's just wood chip the cunt," Willie said.

"Aye, you're right," Jiggs said.

"Fuck it."

At that point, Pinocchio started begging.

"Please, don't kill me. I'll pay you back." And similar shit. Acting like a little bitch. It made little difference. Willie and Jiggs swung him in a chicken 'n wing movement, while Elmer turned the chipper on. They laughed deliriously as he squirmed, but already being a little bored of the situation and having places to be, they let him go and watched him fly high before arcing downwards, straight into the machine. His squeals would have burst most people's eardrums, but the pigs were used to squealing. It took mere seconds for Pinocchio to get pulled down into the blades; the noise he made was incredible. At the end of it, there was a pile of sawdust remaining that the wind picked up. What should have been the life of a magical little boy, had been thrown away and wasted on drugs and petty crime.

No one really died forever in the woods. Pinocchio would respawn somewhere else, but he would never be seen again. The woods were larger than the wildest imagination. You could probably travel a whole lifetime without meeting anyone who had come back. It did not mean that you couldn't die a very painful death. In fact, because most of the residents of the woods had heard about the respawning, most felt death should be painful. It wasn't like dead-dead, so there had to be something done if one deserved to die. The pigs full-heartedly supported the death by pain method and were glad Pinocchio was gone. This would send a ripple of whispers throughout the woods, and by the morning, they would have people breaking down their door to pay them what they were owed. No one would avoid them for a while. It was good business sense.

"Man, that was fun," Willie said.

The other two chuckled in agreement.

"Let's get out of here. There have been some newbie fuckpigs at the bar recently. Let's get down there and get in among that pork," Jiggs said.

As the pigs left to begin their journey to the bar, they were in high spirits. They wouldn't get their money back, but they had always hated that Pinocchio cunt. It just so happened, as they started to walk through the woods, that they came across another character that had been ducking them.

"Humpty fuckin' Dumpty," Jiggs said.

"Well, aren't you a sight for sore eyes?" Willie said as he watched Dumpty turn even more white than usual.

"Guys. I was just coming to find you," Dumpty answered, sounding nervous.

"Oh, you were, were you?" Elmer replied sarcastically.

The pigs knew this had to be a lie. He was weeks late and had even been heard bragging about not paying them down at the pub. Elmer had been banging Rapunzel for a while and she had told him what she had heard when he was last hanging out the back of her. It did nothing for his self-confidence that she was thinking about other things while he was hammering her—balls deep—but the info was needed nonetheless. Apparently, he had gone to see the old witch in the candy house, and she had magically changed his name to Dizzy, but everyone in the woods knew him as Humpty Dumpty. It was said he knew of a way out of the woods, and was bragging he was going to be famous. Not if the pigs had anything to do with it.

"Right, ya egg-shaped cunt! Come here," Willie demanded.

Humpty turned tail and attempted to run, but the stumbling fuck fell arse over head. He rolled onto his back to try and get up, but the pigs were on him. The assault was vicious. All three began raining kicks down on Humpty's rather unconventional body. Every single hit broke him. The pigs' cloven hoofs went straight through the shell. Each time they did, the pigs had to pull their legs back out, but it didn't stop them from getting back up and giving him another kick. Each time a new hole formed, more yolk leaked from Dumpty. A white and yellow slime-like substance ran down the parts of shell that were still intact. It was, in fact, Dumpty's blood. It did not slow the pigs down one little bit. They continued to kick the fuck right out of Dumpty, roaring with laughter the whole time. His eyes had rolled back into his dome-shaped head long before they stopped. A good amount of yolk still remained inside Dumpty, but he was out for the count.

The pigs had barely begun walking back through the woods when they heard the chatter. They recognized a few of the voices.

"Fuckin' dwarfs," Jiggs said.

Each group had been gunning for each other for a while, but they had never come to blows. The pigs knew they were outnumbered, but when it came to fighting, there were only a few dwarfs that would make a difference. They all knew that Sleepy would never make it through a full fight without taking a nap. Bashful wouldn't know where to look. Happy could barely lose his temper for more than a few seconds. Dopey would end up fighting with one of his own team. Grumpy, Doc, and Sneezy were dangerous though. Grumpy was a stone-cold killer, Doc always carried weapons, and Sneezy would often knock people out with an unintended headbutt during a sneeze, or bling someone with his snot before he set about them.

"Let's fuckin' have em," Elmer said, picking up his pace.

"Is that those fucking pigs?" a voice came that sounded like Grumpy.

There was a rustling sound and the dwarfs started to appear through the leaves.

"Well, well, well... If it isn't the three tiny pigs?" Happy said, smiling.

"It's the three little pigs, ya fud!" Elmer retorted.

Grumpy stepped up front, next to Doc.

"We have been looking for you cunts."

"Come and fuckin' get it then. Fuckin' inbreeds," Willie shouted.

The dwarfs and the pigs clashed. A few of the dwarfs went down quick, but others knocked lumps out of the pigs. Punches and kicks flew through the air, and knives were pulled. The first to go down was dopey. He pulled two knives. Willie took one off him, watched him drop the other, and started plugging him quickly with the knife he had taken. He picked the other up as he watched Dopey fall, and turned quickly, tripping over Sleepy. The cunt had fallen asleep. Willie turned around and slit his throat. He was just about to get up when Doc appeared behind him. He smiled down at Willie and then bashed his skull in with a hammer.

The carnage continued as the pigs and dwarfs tried to get one up. The pigs were tough, but the sheer numbers of the Dwarfs caused a problem. Elmer managed to take down Bashful and killed him, jumping on his head—anger overtook him. He got carried away, kicking him in the head, and Grumpy snuck up behind him and wrapped a garrotting wire around his neck, slowly choking the life out of him.

Jiggs stood himself looking at the four remaining dwarfs. Grumpy, Doc, Sneezy, and Happy surrounded him.

"Fuckin' com' on then, ya cunts!" he roared at them and ran straight for Grumpy.

The two began raining blows on each other's faces before the other dwarfs got a hold of him and dragged him to the ground. They held him still while Doc hammered metal spikes through his hands and feet. They crucified him in the dirt. He screamed the whole time about what he was going to do to them if he got away. There was little chance of that. He would be used as a warning. They spent the next few hours cutting little slices into him, watching the blood trickle down his sides, before adding more.

"Skudbooks, fuckin' midgets, inbred cunts." The insults were endless until, eventually, Jiggs was only moaning. After a long time, he passed out. He seemed to still be breathing, but he was done for, so the remaining dwarfs left him and went to see their fallen.

"It's a crying shame. Sleepy, Dopey, and Bashful were good guys," Happy said.

"Yeh, some of the best," Sneezy said before sneezing.

"Fuck 'em. We will replace them tomorrow with three other nuggets. They were useless," Grumpy grunted.

"You're fucking useless," Doc snapped back.

They all knew it was true. When one dwarf died, they would recruit another to take their place. They had to fit the name, so there was often a panel with applicants, and they would pick the most suitable replacement; It was tiresome. People would show up who were too tall, or apply for a position as the new Sneezy, but they never sneezed. Common sense goes a long way, but not many have it.

"Let's just get everything we need to take and get on our way. We can have a good ol' knees-up tonight to remember the lads before they are replaced. Snow White will be fucking raging, so we better get her a few pills to cheer her up," Happy told the others.

"Fuck her. Sick of her shit, anyway. Grumpy old cow."

The others found it ironic that Grumpy should call someone else grumpy, but at the same time, they knew what he meant. She was always like a bear with a sore head when a dwarf had to be replaced, even though she didn't do any of the fucking work. Too busy playing with singing birds and lazing about while all the animals did everything for her. No wonder she was piling on the pounds. There had even been talk of getting rid of her, but the crew was split. Maybe the new lads would sway the numbers.

The four dwarfs buried their comrades where they were, but decided to take Willie and Elmer to eat later. They went on their way and left Jiggs pegged to the ground. He was either out cold or dead. He hadn't moved since they left him. They tied the pigs' legs together and used large fallen branches to carry them over their shoulders—two dwarfs to a pig to make easy work. The dwarfs were workers, but they worked smart rather than hard.

As they went on their way, they hadn't travelled too far before they stumbled across the now deceased Humpty Dumpty. They checked him for life, but it looked like he had bled out.

"Aw, man, do you know what this means?" Happy asked.

"No, what?" Doc replied.

"Ham and fuckin' eggs, my good dwarf," Happy answered.

"Fuck me. I never even thought of that. Ya dancer! Who's got the fuckin' frying pan? Any cunt got beans?" Sneezy asked, sneezing all over Dumpty.

"Will you watch where you sneeze, you daft prick," Grumpy roared.

"Calm down, man," Happy told him.

"I'm not wanting his fucking snotters all through the yolk. The wee dick always wastes our meals. Why is he even allowed near the food anyway?"

"Moany cunt," Sneezy whispered.

"I fucking heard that," Grumpy roared.

Grumpy got to work on the pigs, cutting slices of bacon off them, while Happy got a fire going. They had two frying pans. They scooped egg out of what remained of Dumpty's shell and got the rashers of bacon in the other pan. Doc appeared next to them with a pot of beans.

"Where did those come from?" Happy asked.

"Always got beans with me, kiddo. You never know when you will need them."

Happy had no idea if that was true. The old Doc had been wiped out by The Big Bad Wolf a few months back and they had to find a replacement. The new guy was cool, but none of them really knew him yet.

When the food was cooked, the four dwarfs sat around the fire and had their ham, eggs, and beans.

"Man, that was the dogs' bollocks. Think we should have a rest and then another wee snack before we get moving," Happy said.

"Sounds good to me," Sneezy agreed, feeling somewhat like Sleepy always felt when he was alive.

"Yeh, fuck Snow White. We will get back when we get back," Grumpy added.

"Agreed," was all Doc said.

The dwarfs nattered for a while and eventually drifted off to sleep with their hands on full tummies. As the sun went down, and they snoozed around the fire—with the smell of bacon and eggs still in the air—a shadow appeared in the woods.

Creeping from the trees was a blood-soaked pig. A pig covered in hundreds of tiny slices. He had a hammer in one ruined hand, and a knife in the other. It was only pure adrenaline and force of will that kept him moving. He entered the camp as slowly and quietly as his broken hoofs would allow him. It was a quick, clinical job. Grumpy's skull was smashed in, as was Doc's. Sneezy got his throat slit, and Happy got the knife right through his eye socket.

Jiggs fell back on his ass and passed out again. When he woke up, he was in the shadow of a tall woman. She wore a crown atop her head, but she looked like no queen or princess he had seen before. Every part of his body ached, but his hands and hoofs had been bandaged.

"You are in a bad way, little man," The Wicked Queen said. "We thought you were dead when we came across you. I've heard of you and your brothers. Maybe we could talk. I think our relationship would be mutually beneficial," she went on, giving him her least wicked grin.

"My brothers are gone. It's just me. These fucking dwarfs ambushed us.

"Really? Snow White's Dwarfs, and you killed them all?"

"My brothers and I fought them and killed three. They left after they thought they had killed me, and I came back and killed the rest.

"Yes, I think we can definitely be friends. Come with us and we will get you fixed up. I think you would be happy at the palace. We need to talk more."

Jiggs smiled. He had nothing else to do now. His brothers were gone and, without them, he would struggle to run the drug trade. Certainly not in his current condition.

"Fuck it. I'm in, Queenie," Jiggs answered.

—

AND THAT KIDDIES is where I am afraid we must leave our friends for now. I can't spend much longer looking into the woods without fear of getting stuck there myself. Magic only goes so far. Needless to say, if I was you, and you ever find yourself lost in the woods, don't trust any cunt. It's no fairy tale out there.

The End...

ABOUT THE AUTHORS

M ENNENBACH

M Ennenbach is a poet, a naturalized Texan, a scribbler of tales, a fool, a father.

RUTHANN JAGGE

Ruthann Jagge writes dark speculative fiction and horror. Her stories are influenced by extensive travel, and an appreciation for homegrown horror and superstition. She lives on a rural cattle ranch in Texas with her husband and his animals. Her work is featured in several popular anthologies,and her first solo novella will be published in January, 2022.
Affiliate Member HWA.

www.ruthannjagge.com

NATASHA SINCLAIR

From the heart of Scotland, Natasha finds inspiration to write in just about everything. She doesn't subscribe to boxing art off into a single genre or indeed anything in life — art should be unapologetic in its freedom. Her writing spans genres including speculative, horror, psychological and erotica.
She has independently published, compiled and edited collections and has contributed to several anthologies. She supports other creatives by proofreading, editing, and creating promotional material via Word Refinery services, linked on her site, clanwitch.com
Out-with that, she's an avid gig-goer, reader, vegan, home-educating, nature-loving, adopter of wonky animals.

JASON MYERS

Jason Myers (1983-) grew up in Northwest Ohio. Avid reader for years he put aside his dreams of writing to raise his children and focus on being an EMT/Firefighter. He has been published in horror anthologies as well as several novellas of his own. He is the co-author of the Eternal Sisterhood Series with RJ Roles. RJ and Jason have since founded Crimson Pinnacle Press, a publishing company that deals with horror and the macabre. He currently resides and still serves his city in the fire department in Maumee, Ohio.

RJ ROLES

From 100 word drabbles, to full length novels, RJ Roles is an author that takes pride in his various works of fiction. He is the founder and admin of the Books of Horror Facebook group, and co-founder of Crimson Pinnacle Press with Jason Myers. He lives a quiet life with his wife and many cats in southern West Virginia. Find him on his author page www.facebook.com/groups/AuthorRJRoles or website rjroles.wixsite.com/rjrolesfiction

MATTHEW A. CLARKE

Matthew A. Clarke is a reader and writer of all things bizarro and horror. He has short stories published across multiple anthologies. His latest horror novella, Beyond Human, is set to release in July 2021, and Coffin Dodgers – A bizarro novel, is available now on Amazon. Matthew's influences range from Jack Ketchum and Clive Barker to Junji Ito and Carlton Mellick III. He lives in the South of England with his fiancée, Issy, and a little dachshund called Frank. To find out more about Matthew's work and get the drop on upcoming releases, visit www.matthewaclarkeauthor.co.uk Or www.facebook.com/matthewaclarkeauthor

TARA LOSACANO

Tara Losacano lives in New England with her family and her cat. She is an avid horror reader and has been published in many horror anthologies including Books of Horror Community Anthology vol. 1 and 2, and ABC's of Terror vol. 1 ,2, and 3. She continues to read and write and hopes to publish her own novel soon.

LANCE DALE

Lance Dale was born and raised in Wisconsin and began writing in 2020. His first short story was published in the Books of Horror Community Anthology Vol. 1, and he has been included in several anthologies since. He is an avid fan of extreme metal music, horror movies, and books of all genres. Although he loves writing, he enjoys spending most of his time hanging out with his amazing wife and two children in La Crosse, Wisconsin.

DENISE HARGROVE

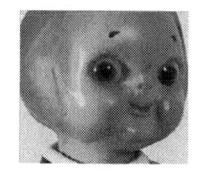

Whether you know her in person, or from one of the various book groups, Denise Hargrove is the quintessential literature enthusiast. Her love of the written word spans all genres, but her heart lingers on true crime, and horror (especially creepy dolls). Though she has written the foreword for the Books of Horror Community Anthologies, this is her first published story. You can find her chasing that old book scent, in search of hidden treasures.

KEVIN J. KENNEDY

Kevin J. Kennedy is the author of Halloween Land and the co-author of You Only Get One Shot, Screechers & Stitches. He has released 3 solo collections of short horror stories and he is one of the UK's most prominent horror anthologists.

He lives in the heart of Scotland with his wife and 3 small fur people, Carlito, Ariel and Luna. You can find him hovering around Facebook most days if you want to chat.

www.kevinjkennedy.co.uk

CRIMSON PINNACLE PRESS

Keep up with all the latest news and projects by joining the Facebook group.

www.facebook.com/groups/crimsonpinnaclepress

This is a work of fiction. Names, characters, places, and incidents either are the product of the author's imagination or are used fictitiously. Any resemblance to actual persons, living or dead, events, or locales is entirely coincidental. Fairy Tale Horrorshow Copyright © 2021 by Crimson Pinnacle Press
All rights reserved. No part of this book may be reproduced or used in any manner without written permission of the copyright owner except for the use of quotations in a book review.

No authors were harmed in the making of this book.

Formatted by J.Z. Foster

First paperback edition 2021
Crimson Pinnacle Press
ISBN (paperback) ISBN (ebook)

Made in the USA
Columbia, SC
14 June 2021